The Poacher's Son

'There are too many wealthy people,' Mr Pooley shouted across the courtroom, 'who have no other means of procuring game, except by purchase. . . . It is at *their* feet we must lay blame. It is *their* habits which necessarily encourage illegal sportsmanship among boys such as Arthur.'

When Arthur's family have almost no money, he follows his father's example and turns to poaching. He enjoys being out in the open far more than being at school, whereas his sister Alice would far rather be in school, learning, than out earning money. For them all, the future looks very difficult.

'A remarkable novel: it has impressed me more than any other children's book in 1982.' *Signal Review*

'An excellent story, beautifully told . . . the style is sensitive and gentle. The appeal of the book lies in the fact that it can be appreciated by children of all ages and background.' *Recent Junior Books*

Rachel Anderson

The Poacher's Son

Fontana · Lions

First published in Great Britain 1982
by Oxford University Press
First published in Fontana Lions 1984
by William Collins Sons & Co Ltd
8 Grafton Street, London W1X 3LA

Copyright © Rachel Anderson 1982

Printed in Great Britain
by William Collins Sons & Co Ltd, Glasgow

to David Hutton

Chapter 1

'PLEASE come all this week. Properly, Arthur!' Alice pleaded. 'The rector's bringing oranges for Empire Day.'

There was to be one orange for every child with good attendance. Oranges were not something we saw more than once a year. So I went with her. The chill spring wind chivvied me along the road. I thought of those oranges, gleaming brighter than the sun. Their brassy image lured me into school every day, and lightened the long walk home.

One orange on Empire Day. Perhaps, I suggested to Alice, there might be some spares? Then, we as were a large family, we might get two? When the calico had been given out at Michaelmas we were given the extra yard on the bolt for little Jenny.

The rector's wife was to hand out the fruit. She waited by Mr Pooley's high desk. It seemed there were no spares, and not even enough to go round the school once. Attendance had been exceptional all week.

The rector snapped his fingers at Mr Pooley to unlock the book cupboard.

'The register will be checked again. Those with fewest attendances will be weeded out.' I was sure that I would be amongst those who were to sit rewardless, orangeless at the back of the class. But, thanks to Alice's persistence in getting me to school all week, I scraped by. Those absences of days on end, when I'd been out in the woods, were on the preceding page of the register.

The rector stood on the other side of Mr Pooley's desk,

and as we filed up, boys in one line, girls in another, to bow or bob to the rector's wife, he delivered one of his talks.

He told us of the country the fruit had come from, of the lowly blackman, blacker than your hat, who had picked them. He told us how God's bountiful goodness had caused the oranges to grow and how his own kindness had provided funds to pay for the oranges. I was interested to hear what kind of trees oranges grew on.

'Please, sir!' I put up my hand. Round us, the trees only gave acorns and beech nuts, food fit for animals, not people. But the rector did not linger on the interesting part of his talk.

'Be quiet, boy, and stay in line.'

He told us that, because we had been given fruit, we were not to get ideas above our station.

'You will realize that, just as I have a duty towards each of you, you have a duty towards your neighbour, to be kind and thoughtful of your neighbour's needs. You must learn to labour truly to get your own living and to order yourself lowly and reverently to your betters.'

We had heard it all before. My brother Humphrey picked his nose. Infants fidgetted. On the bare floor boards beneath one of them, a puddle appeared and spread wide until it reached the feet of one of the big boys. He edged away and sniggered. I didn't mind. I was used to puddling youngsters.

The rector's voice went on. I watched his dark bird eyes darting round down the rows, seeming to peck us up, then spit out our sins and defects like pips in front of us. The words of anger and admonition tumbled out, one after another. I was amazed at how one man's head could contain so many words.

'But above all, God placed each of us where we are in the social order, in the allotted role we have. To envy others or try and change your lot is a sin against the wisdom of God's order, a sin of which I hope and trust you will not be guilty.'

I caught Humphrey's eye and winked. He was still picking his nose. I wondered if the promise of one orange was worth the sermon. I tried to catch Alice's eye. But she was alert to the rector's words. She was so good. I wondered how she could be so good and still strive to be even better.

At last, we were allowed to sing. We thanked the Lord, O thanked the Lord for all his love, and returned to our own benches.

No oranges were eaten. At recess, the yard was filled with fifty golden suns swirling in the air. We tossed them. The girls caught them in their aprons. We rolled them. We played catch. We juggled and caught them. We boys saw how high we could throw them above the school roof.

A pale sun shimmered through the dull day and made the orange skins glow brighter. I was glad that I had endured the sermon. And there was still the promise of the sweet juice and sticky pulp to enjoy.

One boy's orange, thrown too high, unskilfully caught, slipped from his hands and dashed to the ground where it split open. The thin juice ran out like water and mingled with the dirt. Poor Joshua gathered up the pieces, crying. We stood round sympathizing with his loss. Then we envied him as he sucked what he could retrieve of his broken orange. Some were tempted to eat their oranges immediately, instead of taking them home.

We returned to the hall. One spare fruit was left in the crate. I took it out. It was rotten and soft, like green sponge on the underside. I sniffed it and could smell the deep African jungle where it had grown. As I replaced it in the crate, the rector's clawlike hand was over mine.

'Coveting what is not yours, is a sin, you muttonhead.'

'I wasn't taking it, sir. I was smelling it.'

'With the ulterior motive of taking it, no doubt. Very well, since you clearly wish to have *this* fruit instead of your own, you may.' He snatched the good orange from my hand and replaced it with the mouldy one from the crate.

'The children of labourers, I have noticed, are too often in the habit of petty thieving and pilfering. You are accustomed to scrounging for kindling and fuel from the woods and fields and believe yourself entitled, by some common right, to all you see. This is not so!'

'Yes, sir.'

The rector's wife stayed, during the afternoon, to supervize the girls' needlework. Alice was making a needlepoint sampler, the letters picked out in coloured silk cross stitch.

It was a most lovely thing, not grubby and misshapen like some of the girls' work but neat and fresh. Alice let me hold the fabric and I traced round the bright silky letters with my fingers. The words, Alice said, were 'His Light Always With Us'. Beneath the motto she had embroidered a little wreath of flowers.

It seemed a marvel, not only to be able to read and write, but also to sew the words in pink and green. My chance of learning to read grew less every month older that I was. Mr Pooley's special tuition in Dunces' Corner did not seem to help. He held a group of us there while the girls sewed.

All afternoon we worked through the figures from one to twenty, again and again, till I seemed to see figures floating before my eyes.

'Please, please, boy,' Mr Pooley pleaded. 'Couldn't you try a bit harder? The Inspector will be here *any* day now.'

He had pale sandy hair, and a thin yellow beard like a goat. His hands were covered in freckles, like lichen on a rock. I thought he was going to weep like a girl when I got my figures wrong time and again, my fives back to front, my confusion with 12 and 21, with 6 and 9. I wondered if it was worth all the suffering that Mr Pooley and I inflicted on each other, just for one rotten orange.

'Betts, pay attention. What are you dreaming about?'

'My orange, sir.'

'Ah, yes, oranges,' said Mr Pooley. 'Let's try a problem

sum with oranges. How many oranges would it require if there were to be three a week for a year?'

I did not know.

'Work it out in stages, Betts. Firstly, how many weeks are there in a year?'

I did not know. I did not see the world in numbers of weeks. It merged, one season into another, sometimes going backwards a little, so that a bright warm day in March might be followed, not by another bright day, but by a cold winter day, or a mild day in October might be mistaken for June. But the year always caught up with itself in the end, without anybody needing to count the numbers of weeks that passed.

At last, the bell rang for the end of day. We prayed that God would keep our souls safe from harm all night. As we filed out into the yard, the rector, lurking in the porch, pounced on my sister.

'Betts? Are you Alice Betts?'

'Yes, sir.'

He was a big man, with a beaky face and a thin leer like a starling opening its bill.

My sister was never bad. What could she have done wrong to draw attention to herself?

'There is a petty post going for a sturdy country girl, with some relatives of my wife,' said the rector peering down at her. A petty post meant being skivvy in one of the big houses. My sister was too good to be a maid-of-all-work. 'Which I could arrange. They're seeking a bright, intelligent girl like you.'

'Thank you, sir. But I –'

'There's good pay!' the rector enticed her. 'Twenty-five shillings per annum and full board. Your parents would be glad of that, surely?'

'My father's been in employment now for some time on the estate.' There was defiance in Alice's voice. She did not like the rector's insinuation that we were in need of money.

'Besides, my mother wouldn't want me to live away from home yet. She needs my help with the small ones. And I was hoping to stay and take my Standard 6.'

'I can get you a dispensation from the Board.'

'Mr Pooley would like me to stay on too. I know he would.'

The rector's lips tightened. 'Mr Pooley will do what I tell him and what is in the best interest of his pupils.'

'But you see, sir, I was hoping that if I stayed on I might be able to get a scholarship and go on to the grammar school for a year.'

'Grammar school!' the rector repeated, astonished, with a fine spray of spit. His leer had turned to a sneer. 'You? From *this* school?'

'Mr Pooley says I'm bright enough, and I could get a scholarship. Then afterwards, I've heard there is a college where girls may train as schoolteachers. I was hoping . . . maybe . . .' She trailed off.

'Betts, I am deeply disappointed in you. I select you of all the children in this school, for such an opportunity and you've the stupidity and insolence to turn me down!'

The rector looked enraged, picked up his hat, and left the building.

Humphrey had already started for home. Alice and I walked together. A crow flapped languidly across the open field beside us. I threw the remains of my rotten orange at it. It was too rotten even for my Ma to make into marmalade jelly. I only missed by an inch but the crow scarcely wavered off course, and kept on its dead straight line towards the woods behind Keeper's Lodge.

'Why didn't you accept,' I said. 'You must be daft. I would've. Anything to get out of that place. And you *really* peeved him. He'll tell Pooley we've got to learn an extra psalm next week just out of spite.'

We were still a quarter of a mile from home when my dog heard me. She slithered under the big gate and came bounding down the drive towards us. As she leapt up and down licking my face and greeting me with little barks of delight, all my own troubles of the day seemed to dissolve.

'We don't need the rector's money, we're not paupers!' Alice snapped, and walked on. But by the next day our situation had changed so greatly that we did need the money very much.

Chapter 2

*T*HAT night, the mouchers stumbled through the gate onto the estate. It was a still night. If you've any sense, you don't go after roosting pheasants on a still night. They hear you coming. To grab him off his branch, you have to creep up on him upwind, facing into a light breeze.

It was quiet in our kitchen. My Ma and Alice sat at the table to sort hen feathers for mattresses. My Ma tipped them onto a sheet where they lay between them like a mound of flour.

I dozed on the ragmat by the grate. There was red heat on my face, and the tightness of pot roast in my stomach making me forget about my missed orange. I rested my head on my dog's flank so that I could feel her ribcage going up and down as she breathed. I could smell musty dog-smell in her fur. I half opened one eye and watched a dark flea scramble through her fur like a monkey through tall jungle trees.

I loved her differently from the way I loved anybody else, even Alice. My feelings for the dog were matched most closely by my love for my youngest brother, though the dog was more intelligent and more active than poor lolling Jonas who had no strength in his loose limbs, and no sense in his wizened little head.

I half listened to the brief talk as my Ma told Alice not to waste feathers and they would have enough to fill three mattresses. They sorted on in businesslike silence. Feathers don't make noise.

'It's late,' said Alice. 'Pa's not back yet.'

My Ma picked out a stiff wing feather that wouldn't do for sleeping on and threw it aside.

'Poor old hen,' I said. Even during its lifetime, its wings hadn't been much use to it.

'He'll be back when he's ready,' my Ma said. 'He's not a child needing to be fussed after.' It was a reprimand and Alice said nothing. She was old enough to do adult women's work, but she was in no position to order our Pa about as though he were one of the little ones.

The dog's soft body suddenly stiffened under my cheek. She had heard the first sound outside and she was instantly alert. She lifted her head, twitched her snout as though she could listen through her nose.

We heard the metal click as the latch on the big gate was lifted.

'It's Pa,' said Alice, not looking up from her feathers.

She knew it wasn't. Pa didn't use the five-barred gate. None of us did. It was for waggons and carts. Everybody else used the side gate. Children and dogs didn't use any gate at all but bent double and slithered under the gap.

There was a thud like something falling to the ground, then a scuffling, as if that something was trying to scramble to its feet again. My dog's fur stood on end like a hedgehog. She whined and stood up. We heard the high-pitched squeal of the rusty hinge of the gate swinging open. Pa kept that hinge unoiled on purpose, as a warning of intruders.

'There'll be more than one out there,' Alice whispered. '*And* they'll be armed.' Her face had gone nearly as white as the feathers. But I wasn't afraid. The spirit of combat was in me, to get out there and have a go at them.

'The cheeky devils,' our Ma said lightly, as though a gang of armed thieves fumbling in his lordship's woods was quite normal. 'Fancy daring to come in right under our noses! The impudence of it. And in the close season!' In spring the pheasants were to be left alone. And the keepers could get on with rearing. 'They'll be Londoners, and drunk with it, I'll be bound.'

I wondered how she could distinguish a Londoner from any other stranger.

'You can always tell a Londoner by his pasty complexion,' my Ma said shortly. 'And his shrill unpleasant manner of speaking.' Then, as though filling mattresses was far more important than worrying about the mouchers outside, she crossed to the bread-oven, moving gently so as not to disturb the feathers on the table, and put her hand in to test whether it was cool enough now for the first batch of feathers to be baked. Baking in the warm oven cleaned the feathers and killed off the mites. But if it was too hot, it scorched them. A stray wisp of down was caught on the fringe of her shawl. Lifted by a wave of heat from the oven, it unhooked itself and floated to the ceiling.

'I wish Pa were back,' said Alice. It wasn't usual for him to be out so late. Rearing pheasant chicks kept him busy. Once they were old enough to be let out of the coops, they had to be heavily fed to prevent them wandering. 'Those men *know* he's out! They must. Why does he have to be out tonight?'

Our Pa had gone to see about roof repairs at Mr Pooley's place. A gale had blown half the pantiles off his outhouse.

'Help your friends in need, and they'll help you,' said Ma.

I heard the scrunch of feet on gravel. I prised open the shutter and peered through the narrow slit. At first I could see nothing in the dark. Then, I sensed, rather than saw, a whole cluster of men, maybe seven or eight, milling around the gate. A visit from a gang of town thieves excited me. I'd never seen a true villain close up.

There had been a proper battle over some partridges the year before on an estate in the next county. One poacher had been killed, several injured. The constable who tried to arrest them had had his left leg shot.

'Get that shutter closed, Arthur!' Alice said. 'Or they'll see you looking out.'

My bitch slunk over to the back door and growled in her throat. I knew she had scented a strange dog out there.

'There's only one fellow, Alice.' I closed the shutter. 'And it's not you they're after either, so you can stop worrying. He's not stopped. He's going on through.'

Her fear turned to indignation. 'Can't he even *read*?'

There was a painted notice board nailed to a tree by the gate saying what would happen to trespassers.

'Of course he can't read in the dark!' I said. I couldn't read in dark or light but I knew well enough what the board said. It used to give me a sense of authority to stand by the gate pointing up to the board and ordering village children away.

'It's more than trespassing they're after, now isn't it?' said our Ma, and she spread an armful of feathers on a tin baking tray and slid the tray into the oven. From deeper in the wood we heard the geese gaggling excitedly in their pen under the laurel bushes. The mouchers couldn't have visited this estate before or they'd have known about the geese.

Perhaps, I thought with rising excitement, this was the violent gang from the next county, now released from gaol and seeking revenge.

'They'll be after the birds in Great Wood,' I said. 'Shall I go fetch Pa?'

He usually turned a blind eye to villagers poaching the odd rabbit or even picking up a hare. But a professional gang moving in for his lordship's pheasants out of season was another matter.

'No, Arthur!' Ma said sharply. 'You stay here. They're dangerous thugs. On the lookout for trouble. You don't play games with men like that. Anyway it's too far to Mr Pooley's. And your Pa may be on his way back already.'

'He needs warning, specially if they're armed!' Pa had a shotgun with him, but he didn't let fire at anything that moved, like some of the underkeepers. He said you learned more about the whereabouts of vermin and poacher by watching and keeping quiet. Maybe the gang would shoot first.

'Shouldn't I go for Wilkins?' I asked. The Headkeeper's cottage was less than half a mile from ours. I was anxious to get out there and *do* something. So was my dog, keeping up her persistent whine by the door.

Ma hesitated.

'Wilkins ought to be told, especially as Pa's not home,' I said.

'Very well, Arthur. But keep well clear of Great Wood, and come *directly* home. Do you hear me?'

'Yes, Ma.'

'They can't even aim straight.'

I grabbed my jacket and cap, darted to the back door and was through it before she had time to change her mind. As I slammed the door behind me, I heard Alice shriek out. The draught had made the feathers blow all about. I heard my Ma call after me:

'And it's not Wilkins, remember. It's *Mister* Wilkins to you!'

I didn't like Wilkins, the headkeeper, and he didn't like me. Yet I had to call him 'Mister', while he could call me anything he pleased and often did. He didn't care for boys, even the eldest sons of underkeepers. No child, so he believed, could be trusted not to trample through the woods.

'You disturb the young pheasant. You steal eggs. You cause more damage to his lordship's game than all the weasels and crows and rats put together.'

He was a married man with a son of his own, yet Wilkins preferred his underkeepers to be bachelors, unencumbered by wives and children.

I ran across the yard, fetched my catapult from the hook in the shed, and sprinted all the way to the Wilkins' cottage without once stopping on the way. I put my personal dislike of him out of my mind. It was, after all, thanks to Wilkins that my father had employment. And it was thanks to employment that we had a warm home, a full cooking pot, and all the firewood we needed. I knew that I owed Wilkins, *Mister* Wilkins, my full loyalty.

Just thinking about my splendid loyalty warmed me and made me feel better about his small angry eyes, and his large nose, red-veined from being out in all weathers.

My dog ran beside me, delighted to be out on a night adventure.

Wilkins was not home.

'Already set out,' said his wife through the window. 'Calling up the undermen. They'll deal with the intruders sharpish.' It sounded to me as though there was going to be some good fun. 'So you'd better hurry straight back home,' said Mrs Wilkins, wagging her finger. 'And keep that bitch of yours on a leash. My husband's warned you before now, hasn't he? You boys have no respect.'

'Yes ma'am,' I said. I took my belt from round my waist and made to seem as though I were about to use it as a leash on my dog's collar. But as soon as I was beyond her garden gate, I put it back. Although she was only a mongrel crossbreed, I had trained my dog to be as well-mannered and obedient as even one of Mr Wilkins' pointers. Besides, how did Mrs Wilkins think a boy could run properly if his trousers were about to fall down?

I followed the boundary wall home. My eyes became more accustomed to the darkness. I suddenly had the excellent idea of proving my loyalty to Wilkins by helping him find the moucher gang. First I had to locate them accurately myself.

I changed direction, the dog keeping close to my heels, and I jogged back towards Great Wood, towards the tall beech trees beyond the goose pens. Whether in darkness or bright sunlight, I could make my way silently through the woods. I knew every inch of this tangled undergrowth. I knew when to duck for a low branch, when to step quietly over a bumpy tree root, where to avoid the crackling of twigs underfoot. I would sometimes stalk my Pa when he went on his evening rounds of the coops. It was a dangerous game, for Pa's gun was loaded in case he should see a cat, a magpie, or some other predator of the young chicks. But if *he* was a good shot, *I* had learned to be an even better stalker. I could glide invisibly between trees, and blend into the brambles. My dog knew when to creep, when to stand motionless like the stone dogs on his lordship's terrace.

I found the mouchers without difficulty. They were certainly not stealthy about their night business. They were arguing in hoarse whispers while their two ill-trained lurchers bounded noisily through the bracken, sniffing this way and that, chasing invisible game and imaginary rabbits. No sane rabbit would be out of its burrow after the warning this gang had given.

There was no sign of Wilkins. If I went in search of him I might miss out on the fight. I decided that I might as well have a few shots at them myself. They were incompetent and, according to my Ma, probably drunk, whereas I was agile, young, and sober. I knew that I stood an excellent chance of scoring several hits from the shelter of darkness, and thereby gaining Wilkin's gratitude. Mr and Mrs Wilkins' son, a few years older than I, had once caught a solitary poacher red-handed. Wilf Wilkins had been rewarded by his lordship himself, with a guinea.

I took my catapult from my pocket, and a smooth fair-sized pebble and aimed for the neck of the man whose back was nearest me. To my surprise, I saw that my pebble must have hit him full on the neck, for he yelped, lost his balance and toppled sideways to the soft floor of leaves with a quiet curse.

To my further astonishment, instead of getting back to his feet, he seemed to disappear from sight altogether, as though the ground had swallowed him up. This, in a sense, is what had happened. Before I had even time to select another flint from my pocket and take aim for a shot at a second man, there was a crashing and crackling of dry branches. Another rogue fell backwards and disappeared into the ground. Three men in all, and one lurcher, tumbled into the pit which had been dug underneath the pheasants' favourite roosting tree. From its earthy depths came the roars and shouts of confusion and drunken pain, combined with the flapping and squarking of frightened birds as the dog not in the pit snapped excitedly at the long tail-feathers.

I patted my dog on the back and whispered encouragement. 'Go there, girl! Go get.'

She bounded obediently through the undergrowth and took up a stand, snarling at the edge of the pit, seeming far fiercer than she really was, and prevented the trapped men from climbing out. They continued to roar while the others ran off, straight into the arms of Wilkins, five farmhands, several underkeepers, and the police constable.

I stayed quietly in my hiding place and enjoyed a good view. In the entire fight, there was only one shot fired, though in the confusion I didn't see who fired it.

The ruffians didn't seem nearly so dangerous once they were tied up. The constable kept beating one of them about the legs and head with his truncheon, even though the man was sobbing.

'Stealing! Robbing what's not yours to take!' he screamed, and continued to knock the man nearly senseless. Since it was the same fellow who'd been victim to my catapulted flint on the back of the ear-lobe, I felt almost sorry for him.

'We was only out for a bit of fun,' another of them whined, a big man in a bright checked waistcoat. 'We didn't mean no harm.'

But they had the tools of their crime with them, a gun, their two ill-trained dogs, a net and a sack.

One of the farmhands was ordered by Wilkins to beat

through the undergrowth with his stick to see if there were any more men hiding. The farmhand beat savagely and seemed in a vicious mood, no doubt from having been called by Wilkins from his cosy fireside. As he swung his heavy staff closer and closer to my hiding place, I abandoned my earlier idea of revealing myself and claiming recognition for having bravely knocked the first poacher into the pit.

Instead, I retreated quietly through the trees. I didn't whistle up my dog since this would give myself away. I knew she'd follow of her own accord as soon as she realized I had gone.

Once out of earshot, I ran quickly home before my Ma should notice how long I had been away.

I was already upstairs and in bed, apparently asleep beside my brother Humphrey, before the villains, guarded by Wilkins' men, passed along the drive beside our lodge, and down to the constable's cottage to be charged.

'There must have been four or five more as got away,' I heard Wilkins say. 'But any rate we got their dog.'

Next morning, my Pa found the dog that Wilkins had shot. She was on the beech leaves in the wood, still only half-dead. She was not the poachers' dog.

The shot had gone clean through the base of her spine. She lay on her side staring at the trees, with dull but conscious eyes. She made a little whine of friendship when she saw me, and moved her front paw.

My Pa finished her off quickly with a blow from the flat of his spade, and dug a hole under the trees and buried her.

I couldn't cry. Grown boys of my age don't make tears that show. But later that morning I watched Alice weep for me. Her tears tumbled onto the yellow calico as she sat in the yard and sewed the mattress covers.

'You loved her, didn't you?' she snuffled, and wiped her eye with the cloth.

I nodded. Till now, I hadn't realized how much I took her for granted.

'There'll be other puppies for you,' Alice said, to console herself as well as me. 'To take her place.'

I shook my head. There could never be another dog like that.

But the loss of my dog that morning was as nothing compared to the greater losses which were to come to all of us by evening.

Wilkins called at Keeper's Lodge. He knocked, not at the back, but at the front door. Nobody ever came by the front, unless it was for something formal. My Ma and I had to shift the box of seed potatoes, some mole-traps, a coil of rope and the trunk for blankets, all of which were stored up against the front door, in order to open up and let Wilkins in. He stood sternly before our fire, warming his backside, while Ma went out the back to find Pa. He was out in the sheds, grinding up a mess of grain, egg-shell, and skim milk for the chicks' meal.

Alice and I crouched on the stairs, our ears pressed to the wooden wall.

I had a hope that Wilkins had heard about my involvement in the previous night's battle, and had come to thank Pa for my help. But this was unlikely. Wilkins never thanked anybody. Then, I thought that he had at any rate come to apologize about killing my dog.

It was neither of these. We heard Mr Wilkins ask why our Pa had not been home the previous evening. We heard Pa explain about going up to Mr Pooley's.

Alice gulped. Mr Wilkins surely was not going to accuse her hero, the schoolmaster, of being involved in poaching?

'Since when has roof-repairing been your job, Betts?'

'It is not my job, sir. I was doing a friend a good turn. He has been very good to my Alice, lending her books and the like.'

'A friend, eh? And doing another friend the good turn of not being on duty where you are employed to be. Most conveniently for him, and inconveniently for his lordship.'

The interview did not seem to be going well for Pa. But he never got angry. He never said anything about the terrible state Mr Pooley's roof was in. His home, next to the school, was kept in very poor condition. The School Governors left all repairs as long as they could. But Pa didn't say any of this. He just answered Yes sir, or No sir, speaking slowly and so softly that at times we could hardly hear him. Wilkins, on the other hand, spoke loudly and clearly so that the wooden panels, against which our ears were pressed, vibrated.

'Roof-mending in the dark?' Wilkins snarled.

'No, sir,' said Pa. 'I inspected the roof before dark, sir. I would not attempt to mend in the dark.'

'And so you immediately returned home to attend to your work as underkeeper?'

'No, sir.'

'Maybe then, you returned instead to admit those ruffians to the estate, to warn them of the pit?'

The relentless and insolent questioning went on and on, round and round in circles and always back to the same point. Pa was a big man, and could easily have struck Wilkins down with a blow of his arm. But he was gentle too, with soft pale eyes and yellow hair the colour of summer straw.

'No, sir, I did not return home. I stopped for a sup of beer in the schoolmaster's kitchen, offered out of friendship, for he wished to talk to me.'

'Mr Pooley, an educated man, wished to talk to *you*?'

'He wished to ask me about my daughter Alice, sir. He has some notion about her doing the scholarships. He was onto persuading me.'

'And you talked about scholarships all evening,' Wilkins said with a leer.

There was no evidence against our Pa, but he lost the job all the same. Somebody had to be held responsible.

'I said they'd find something to pin on me, now didn't I!'

said our Pa with a laugh after Wilkins had gone. 'That business about the old vixen.'

Pa had once set a gin-trap for a troublesome fox. But his lordship, besides being a game-shooting man, was a fox-hunting man.

'And he didn't care to see a fox, which he might have hunted with the hounds, caught up in a keeper's snare!'

We were ordered to vacate Keeper's Lodge within the fortnight.

So we set out, with all our possessions piled high on a borrowed handcart, and none of us with any idea where in the world Pa was leading us.

Chapter 3

I CLOSED the gate behind us for the last time and Ma began to cry. That started Alice off. Then spindly-legged Jonas, lying on the verge, began to wail, though he can't have known why.

Pa lifted him onto the handcart and propped him up against the new feather mattresses.

It was a dismal procession. At its head, Humphrey and I glumly helped Pa to push the cart. Only our little Jenny chattered gaily at the excitement and interest of it all. She had hardly been off the estate in her whole life, except to the font to be baptized when she was born. She gathered a posy of deadnettle and dandelions from the side of the road.

Ma, weighed down with a basket on each arm, stopped and mopped at her face with the corner of her apron.

'The shame of it!' she said. 'We were always an upright family. I don't come from working stock. What'll the village say? What'll we live on? What will we eat?'

'*Some*body has to be scapegoat,' said Pa and he shrugged his broad shoulders. Then he grinned. 'It sets their record straight. And it would never be the magistrate himself taking the blame, now would it, though there's more than one pheasant been laid on *his* doorstep. Wilkins never did care for me. Ever since, well anyhow I dunno why.'

'I'll bet it was that Joseph Plumb got you muddled up with all that,' said Ma with a suspicious sniff. 'He's a scoundrel.'

'It was not,' said Pa. 'Jo Plumb's a loner.'

'You sure you weren't in with them mouchers, George?'

she asked. She had been cold and hard towards our Pa ever since.

Pa stopped the handcart, put his arm round Ma's shoulder and gave her a squeeze. 'No, Elsie love. Cross my heart and hope to die, I promise you I weren't.'

We trundled on down towards the village.

'Not this time anyhow,' he added with a wink, 'though I'm not saying as I weren't never where I oughtn't to be.' But Ma was busy consoling Jonas. He'd slumped sideways and banged his head against an empty tea-can.

Passing through the centre of the village was the worst part of the journey. Many afternoons, that main street is quite deserted, except for a dog sunning itself, or a duck waddling to the pond. But today of all days it seemed as though every living soul was out and about, running an errand, or taking the air on their doorstep, or seeing to their front garden. Each looked round to watch us trudge past. And I knew, and Alice knew, and Ma knew that no sooner were we out of earshot than they'd be scurrying about.

'I'll *not* be gossiped about,' Ma said under her breath.

Pa nodded to some of his acquaintances. Few returned the greeting. Most turned away as though they hadn't heard. Yet whenever they had wanted a tip-off about where the next big shoot was to be, so they could sneak elsewhere and catch a rabbit for the pot, they were as friendly as could be. It costs nothing to be friendly to a gamekeeper and you may even gain some advantage. An ex-keeper is another story. Now we were nothing, just one more family of the unemployed.

A taggle of children joined on behind us, chanting and giggling, as though following a troupe of travelling gipsies. I knew one of them from the rare days when I attended school. I gave her a kick with the hard toe of my boot. She stopped chanting.

We turned up the narrow lane towards Pit Bottom. Alice's face seemed to crumple. Her spirits sank lower.

There was only one place in the world where Pa could be leading us. And everybody who had watched us push through the village now knew to what depths we had sunk.

Halfway up the lane, Pa paused to wait for little Jenny. She lagged behind, her short stumpy legs already tired out. He went back for her and gathered up her, and her trailing bouquets. Then he picked up the whimpering Jonas and strode up Pit Bottom Lane with his felt hat pushed jauntily to the back of his head, and a child on each arm, whistling to himself.

He looked more like a man setting out on a harvest picnic than a father of five without work, home or prospects. He kept up his merry whistling while Ma kept up her wailing and sniffing.

Humphrey and I had to push the handcart without Pa's help. It was heavy. The wooden wheels caught in a rut and the whole cart tipped sideways. It was lucky Jonas was no longer on it or he'd have slithered off into the ditch. As it was, two pans and a bucket toppled off. Alice ran to pick them up and helped us straighten the cart.

The lane was narrow at the top and steeply rutted. The hawthorn grew high and unkempt. We passed a tumbledown hovel, half hidden behind overgrown elder trees.

'Old Mrs Craske lives in there,' Alice whispered. 'Widow. Never seen in the village, ever.'

Alice always knew what was what about everything, for she went to school quite regularly.

'Except for confinements,' Alice hissed. 'And for the laying out of the body, after a death.'

Humphrey lowered his head, gripped the wooden handle more tightly and pushed on to pass the widow's house as quickly as possible.

A little way beyond, Pit Bottom Lane petered out into a dead end. At last, we were there.

'Where's the pit then?' said Humphrey.

But there was no pit, nor ever had been, just more woods

and fields stretching away, and before us the meanest, dampest, mouldiest home that any family could wish to live in.

We stared through the hedge.

'Oh, but it's awful!' gasped Alice. 'We can't! Not in *there*!'

'At five shillings a year we most certainly can,' said Pa, nudging open the ricketty gate with his knee.

'But an old man *died* in there!' Alice said. 'His wife went mad and got put in the workhouse. He was left all alone and died!'

I felt quite glad that I went to school so seldom, for it seemed as if the fear of death was what Alice had chiefly learned.

'There's plenty places where people have died, Alice,' Pa said gruffly. 'And it don't mean you can't live in them after. People are living and dying all over the world.'

Ma gazed at her new home with her red puffy eyes, unable to speak. At last she said, 'Alice is right. We've reached the bottom, George. The very rock bottom. It's nothing but a byre, a cow-byre.' She began to weep again.

Humphrey glanced at me, and rolled his eyes upwards in mock disapproval. I pretended not to notice, for you have to show some loyalty to your Ma even if she has been crying like a baby all week.

The cottage, or cow-byre, or barn or whatever it was, stood on a narrow strip of land, backed by a dense wood of young trees. The low mud walls seemed as though they were about to collapse under the weight of the huge, wet, sodden thatch. At one end, the reeds were over-grown with ivy, in the middle it sprouted a crop of self-seeded rye grass, and at the far end it was sparse and balding where birds and mice had burrowed for their nests. You could see the roof-beams showing through like old grey bones.

In the garden, if it could be called that, deep grass and brambles, tangled old ones from last year and new strong ones from this, and last summer's dead rose-bay stalks taller than Pa's hat, grew right up to the door.

'Nothing a good scything won't put right,' said Pa. He immediately set down the little ones in the ragged grass, seized the scythe from the handbarrow and stripped bare a pathway up to the door. Then he took his shovel from the handcart, strode back down Pit Bottom Lane a few yards and, from the hedgerow, dug a wild briar rose which he had spotted as we came up. He planted the briar stock beside the door and beckoned Ma up the scythed path.

'There, my sweet Elsie,' he said, took off his hat, and bowed low to her. 'Your own rose garden, just right for the fine lady you are. And by next summer them blooms'll be rioting all over the place.' He pushed open the creaky door. 'Enter the palace of your dreams, my love,' he said and kissed her cheek.

A house martin swooped out through the door between them.

'Seems somebody else moved in before us,' Ma said with a sniff and almost laughed.

Inside, the cottage stank of misery and animal droppings. It was both damp and stuffy at the same time. The ivy growing over the windows blocked out light and air. It was furnished with a rough table, a scrap of yellow lace over the windows, and little more. We had had to leave our fine oak dresser behind.

'But it'll be the grandest home you ever saw, once we get it right,' said Pa, encouraging us with a smile and a pat on the back. 'Nice and independent, and far from the snooping village.'

'And a good long way from the pump too!' said Alice. 'You won't get me carrying buckets all the way up from the village.'

'There's plenty of good rainwater in the tub,' said Pa.

Once she had set us to work, our Ma seemed to cheer up. Working was the one thing she lived for. So we worked alongside her like slaves. We had to make the place habitable before nightfall. Only Jonas did not help. We left him lying on the ground outside, till someone remembered to bring him in.

Humphrey and I inspected the water-tub when we went out to collect kindling from the copse behind the house. The water was dark and slimy and wriggling with red threadworms.

When Alice and I unloaded the family goods off the handcart onto the stone floor, I discovered how much of what I had always thought of as Pa's own, had not been his at all, but belonged to the estate, or was on purchase-loan. Pa's dogs I knew were not his own to keep, for they had been returned to the kennels. Nor, I now saw, were the two shot guns, nor the gun-rack that used to hang on the kitchen wall. Nor the wooden case of cartridges which had lived under his bed at Keeper's Lodge. The store of copper-snares which hung on a peg in the shed had not been his, though I noticed half a dozen of them now, under our grey blankets when I bundled them up, to carry indoors.

They had let Pa keep his boots and gaiters since they could hardly send him away barefoot. But his best brown velvet jacket and breeches, which he wore for the big shoot when ladies and gentlemen came from all over the country had not, after all, been his own.

'I hope the new keeper has Pa's same measurements,' said Humphrey. I giggled too at the thought of a small lean man, hung about in brown velveteens built for Pa's great size.

Alice didn't laugh.

'At any rate, he'll be enjoying Pa's vegetables,' she said bitterly. Pa had been proud of his plot at Keeper's Lodge. People even used to come up from the village to hang over the fence by the *No Trespassing By Order* sign and admire the neat rows of green, the fine tilth, the beans which were always ready just a little earlier than other men's.

I felt sorry for Alice. Like our Ma, she minded when

things weren't just right. Whenever she wasn't studying at school, or at home trying to teach me to study, then she was hard at work helping with the scrubbing and washing and cooking to keep things just right.

Pa could not get the fire to light. The grate was cold, the kindling damp, and the chimney so full of holes that it would not draw properly.

We had bread and cold water for supper. Ma strained the water through a muslin cloth and in the dark you couldn't see how murky it was.

We went up to bed straight after. There was nothing to stay up for. In the sloping roofspace at the top of a crooked stairway were two rooms so low you could scarcely stand upright. In them were three rickety beds for the seven of us. There was no way of telling in which one the previous occupant had died.

Ma and Pa took Jonas in with them behind the partition. And in the other room, Alice and Jenny shared one bed, Humphrey and I the other. Through the bare patches, the thatch was open to the sky so you could see stars. I liked the feeling that we were sleeping almost outside. But I could hear from the tossing and muttering in the other bed that Jenny and Alice did not. Nor Humphrey. He cuddled up close to me, and asked to hold my hand. He was less afraid of the old man who had lived and died, perhaps in the very bed we now lay on, than of our neighbour, Mrs Craske, midwife and caretaker of the bodies of the dead. He was frightened that she might choose to visit us. He put his arms round my neck and clutched so tightly that I thought he was going to throttle me.

'She might be a witch. And fly in when we're asleep and eat us.'

It seemed to me we were more like to see another house-martin, or a barn owl, flitting in through the holes, than an old woman.

As he fell asleep, relaxing his iron grip round my neck, a

black darting shape swooped in low past our heads. For an instant, I too was very scared. But it was a bat.

Long after the others were asleep, I was kept awake by the rustlings and scrabblings of small creatures overhead. I liked the sound of their company. The poor things were probably more startled by our arrival, than we were of them.

In the morning, our new mattress covers were splattered with grey bat-droppings, and Pa was already up on the beams overhead, filling in the bare patches with a makeshift thatch of dried bracken and straw. His face appeared in one of the holes above us.

'Good morning, children!' he said and then filled in the last holes, and the loft was plunged into a grey half-light. But at least it was now nearly waterproof.

It seemed to me strange that it was all because of going to see about mending Mr Pooley's roof that our Pa ended up here, having to mend his own rotten roof with bracken. I tried to talk to Alice about how odd it was, but she was edgy and snapped, 'Idle thoughts like that never brought anybody any good.'

I think she was upset about having so many bat-droppings on the new calico, right where she and Jenny's heads lay.

Ma said, 'We'll light a fire with damp leaves this evening and try to smoke them out.'

Straight after breakfast, Pa put on his jacket and braces and waistcoat, ready to go to town. It was nine miles to Reepham Market. He had some bread for his dinner in one pocket, and in the other, he put Ma's clock, carefully wrapped in a clean handkerchief.

'But that's Ma's clock!' I said. 'You can't take that!'

It had always stood on the dresser at Keeper's Lodge. It had a square blue face and silver hands, but it didn't keep time.

Pa nodded.

I wondered why he did not take something of his own, instead of the one possession that our Ma owned. His gun would have been worth a good deal more than a clock-case without any workings inside, however pretty its face.

'You gave it to her!' I said.

He had bought it for her at a travelling fair.

'And now I'm having to take it back,' he said, and he strode out of the door without another word. He didn't even turn to say goodbye.

I looked at my Ma, at the way she was letting him walk off with it.

'He's wrong,' I said, 'to take it. He should have taken something of his own.'

'He doesn't have anything.'

'But he *does*.' I knew he still had the shotgun. I had seen it on the handcart.

'Pa says my clock'll fetch a good price, with that silver on it. He's a sensible man. A good organizer. When he's through with paying the rent, he knows we'll be safe for a year, till things come right.'

'It was *your* clock.' I remembered how lovingly she used to dust it. She probably felt about that clock like I felt about my catapult. Just to feel it in my pocket made me safe. It was almost part of me.

'Stop going on about it, Arthur. I'll be too busy what with living here even to think about it. In fact, I wouldn't be thinking about it if it weren't for you. Now be a good lad and go and fetch in the water.'

When he was underkeeper, Pa went to town once a year for the big show, and to be fitted for his velveteens. Now, as then, Ma let us wait up for him to get back.

He was late, sweeping in out of the night like a magician, laden with all the wonders and excitements of the city. The first thing we saw was the great sack of meal which he had carried on his back all the way up from the crossroads where the carrier had set him down. And he had a silver trinket from the market for our Ma. He fastened it round her neck.

'And I won't never take it away to sell or pawn, as long as I live,' he said. 'That's a promise to you, Elsie.'

Our Ma wasn't ever much good at saying thank you or looking pleased, but you could tell she was, by the way she kept patting it to make sure it was still there.

Pa also brought back a currant bun for each of us. Their rounded tops were brown and shiny with baked-in sweetness and the currants were black and swollen. And he had a seven pound packet of tea.

'Seven pound of tea! The extravagance. George, why d'you *do* these things?' said our Ma.

Pa explained how he had found a tea merchant's where tea was selling a penny cheaper than in our village store, so it was an economy.

He also had four ounces of nails to patch up the rafters, and a packet of dried fruit, not dry and gritty like the candied peel in the village which we sometimes had, but juicy and glistening with sugar.

'So we're well set up for the future then,' said Pa, and Ma gave a quick nod of approval as she put away the tea in the dark back of the cupboard, like a squirrel hoarding nuts, and the change from Pa's spree in the money-jar. Pa also had four ounces of lead shot wrapped in a twist of brown paper, for refilling empty cartridges. But he didn't show us that.

While we ate the currant buns, Ma breaking off pieces for Jonas and feeding them to him, Pa told us about the bustle of the market, the noise of the traffic, the bright shops, the scurrying crowds of people, the runaway horse and the One Man Band with the performing monkey dressed in real clothes. I didn't think I would like to go to town, though I did like to hear about it.

The day after his trip, I saw Pa rub over the muzzle and lock of his gun with a paraffin rag, then polish it with another rag. Then he wiped over the breech with the same oily rag so that the swirly grain of the old walnut glowed.

Finally, I saw him carefully wrap the gun in a piece of sacking and slide it under the eaves of the cottage. He rearranged the reeds and ivy so that nothing showed.

'Will you sell it when the clock-money's run out?' I asked.

He turned round, startled. He didn't know I was there. He shook his head. 'My uncle gave me that gun. It's like a symbol.'

'Why d'you hide it?' My Pa was an open man with no need of secrets.

'No point in having it lying around is there, like an open advertisement? Anyhow, I don't have no licence. We've got to be even more law-abiding now than ever we were. You hear that.'

'But would you sell it, when the money runs out?'

'We'll wait and see about that when the time comes,' said Pa. 'I dare say your Ma can take in a bit of washing if need be. Now you get along and help your brother with the digging.'

He added, more as an afterthought to himself, 'And I don't have no powder yet neither.'

I took up the spade and went to the top end of the garden to join Humphrey in the sweaty struggle to create a smooth bed of fine earth where at present there was a matted growth of ground elder and dead nettle. It was a battle of boys against nature, a race against time, to get seeds planted, and catch up on the early spring. For we had left behind four rows of sown broad beans, and sprouts, leeks and the leafy tops of the early-crop potatoes. When the year was already well on, we must start again from the beginning. But if Humphrey and I could prepare the ground, Pa could at least get in main-crop potatoes and cabbage.

I pulled off my jacket the better to dig, then my shirt too. The sun shone down on our backs as we dug. Alice brought us out a can of cold tea. A blackbird chortled in the hawthorn as though laughing at us for having to work.

Little Jenny toddled out to watch us. We hacked away at

the heavy soil more furiously than ever, so that she could see what fine brothers we were. Great clods of earth, chips of broken brick, fat pink earthworms, beetles, thick gnarled dandelion roots, all were vigorously heaved up.

My heart seemed to burst with cheerfulness. There was a job of work to be done. Our home was good. The money jar was full, our future settled. Life at Pit Bottom wasn't going to be bad at all.

Or so it might have been if there hadn't been school to which I seldom went. Some days I explored the woods. Others, I went further afield and took a day's stone-picking or half a day's swede-trimming. Just when the spring weather was at its best, they had to find out about my truanting.

Chapter 4

THERE was a sick heavy feeling in my stomach when I heard the sound of that mournful bell tolling out across the fields. It was like a death sentence. I couldn't face the bread and dripping Ma had set out for breakfast. But with Pa home, there was no chance to feign illness.

Slowly, reluctantly, I took up my dinner and my two-pence for Mr Pooley, my penny for the slate and my halfpenny for the pencil, and set out with Alice and Humphrey. It seemed madness to spend good money paying for me to go where I didn't want to be. I kicked at the new grass springing up in the lane. I walked slower and slower. The school bell seemed to clang faster and faster.

Alice waited for me to catch up and then pulled my arm. 'Please keep up, Arthur! We'll be late. You know Mr Pooley hates us being late.'

It was against Governor's rules to be late. Lateness was marked against your name in the black book, and the Governors saw it. The rector was a Governor. So was his lordship, though he didn't go to Governors' meetings. He was always busy.

'You go on, Alice. I'll catch up,' I said and stopped altogether. Four rooks circled overhead and then moved lazily towards the thicket behind our cottage. They seemed to beckon me.

'*No! Please*, Arthur. You know you won't,' Alice begged.

I didn't want to disappoint her. I didn't want my name entered in the black book. But still less did I want to suffer a whole dragging day's boredom, a whole seven hours of frustration and humiliation in that stuffy overcrowded hall, sitting on the bench with tiny children half my size, always being shown up for the dunce.

A soft wind ruffled the wheat seedlings in the field, and white spring clouds drifted swiftly across the sky so that the dark landscape was broken with sudden streaks of brightness.

'Why must I?'

'You know perfectly well why!' said Alice sharply. She sounded for a moment like our Ma. 'Because it's the law.'

There hadn't been a law when my Pa was a boy. He had been free to leave school when he was twelve.

'And so you can learn to *read*.'

For six years, Mr Pooley had been trying. Alice was still trying. But there was no reason why, after all this time, someone should suddenly be able to teach me now.

'You know I don't need to. I'm going to be a keeper when they let me leave. Pa didn't read.'

Why should I still have to waste my days in school? Mr Wilkins' son had already been apprenticed to a keeper on a nearby estate. Why couldn't I?

Alice finally gave up persuading me. I watched her hurry on down the lane, leaping and skipping over the campion. As the death-knoll stopped, I saw her take Humphrey's hand and they ran helter-skelter towards the village. I knew that I could trust her. She would make some excuse.

'He's sick today, sir. He's needed home helping with the heavy work. Dad won't have the twopence to spare this week, sir. He's got no boots, sir. He's gone tatering, sir.'

They were all excuses made by other children, less fortunate than ourselves.

I skirted the edge of the wheatfield and saw a partridge hen followed by four of her young, bobbing between the green stalks. Then up to Pit Bottom wood behind our cottage. All the country around here had to be explored and

33

discovered so that I could know every branch, every distorted limb, every hollow and grassy path so that I could hold them as my own, just as I had possessed Great Wood.

As I entered the wood, I broke through a new web spun between two bushes. It was so fine I could not see it and it was only as I felt the invisible stickiness stroke against my cheeks and saw the blowflies dangling in mid-air, that I realized I had destroyed the spider's food source. I climbed a young oak on the edge of the wood, settled myself comfortably into the curved arm of the tree to listen, to watch, and to become part of the life of the wood. A woodpigeon, startled by my arrival, settled down again on the branch immediately above to preen. So long as I stayed still, there was little chance that he would see me. A pigeon, once perched, rarely looks straight down.

From that height, I could see right across the fields as far as the village, where the low blueish shapes of the dwellings and the church and the school stood out against the brown and green of the fields.

I wondered if perhaps Humphrey was standing in for me, to call out for me when the register was taken. He had done so before now, answering to both his name and mine so that my absences – as recorded in the black book – did not seem quite as many as really they were. With nearly forty children in his care, from little'uns of barely five years, up to big boys of going on fourteen, Mr Pooley was often confused.

Humphrey was three years younger than me, but I was small for my age and we both had the same bright hair and red cheeks. Many people took us for the same person, so long as they didn't see us together.

I looked away from the village and back up into the wood. Already Humphrey could read and write better than I could. He had passed his Standard 3 last year. Perhaps he would end up with brains as good as Alice, and then, like her, he might become a teacher. If that happened, I should certainly be proud of him, but it wouldn't make me envy him.

With my catapult, I shot a crow for sport. I picked up the corpse and fastened it to a fence, alongside six dead weasels whose shrivelled skins flapped in the breeze like grey washing.

I watched a kestrel hover, sizing up a creature in the rough grass below. It plummetted like a dropped stone, caught nothing and within moments, was up again, quivering in the same spot, as though that piece of sky was visibly marked. It waited and swooped four times before it finally caught its prey and made off to the privacy of the woods.

All day, sounds of school drifted up from the village. At intervals, I heard the shouts of children released into the yard, the slam of a door, a distant wavering of a handbell, then silence. At school, children had to do everything by the bell, whether or not they were ready. Here, time did not rule my day. When I was hungry, I dropped down from the tree, like the kestrel to the ground, and found a place to eat. Our dokey on schooldays was always the same. Two pieces of bread spread thickly with dripping. It tasted rich and salty and, though not as filling as a proper hot meal, the pork taste reminded you of the supper you had had the night before, and more important of the hot meal you were going to get in the evening.

The poor prisoners in school had to eat their dokey sitting at their desks. I ate mine in the comfort of an old hayrick. If they were thirsty, they had to ask permission to go out to the pump.

I lay down on the grass and drank from the stream. I trailed my hands amongst the weeds, I tried to catch water-snails on a blade of grass. I smelled the sweet smell of crushed watercress that grew all along the bank.

I didn't like its sharp mustardy taste, but Ma and Pa did, so I gathered a big armful to give to them. Then I remembered, and threw it back into the stream and watched it drift away downstream like a green swan's nest. To take it back would show where I had spent the day.

It had been a good day, as were all days spent in the woods. I was cheerful and confident as I made my way back across the fields to meet up with Alice and Humphrey on their way home from school.

Pit Bottom was isolated, I did not have to be as careful to keep myself hidden as I used to be round Keeper's Lodge. Without even checking to see if the lane was deserted, I slithered down through a gap in the blackthorn and tumbled onto the track.

I could not have chosen my moment worse. The lane was not deserted.

I thought for a moment, I hoped, that the dark figure, scruffy and mottled-black like a starling, might have his back towards me and be striding *away* down the lane. But I could see his eyes, dark and beady, swivelling. And he was coming directly towards me, the Bible under his arm. My heart stopped beating as I hesitated, wasting precious seconds. I would run for it, make a clean getaway before he should see who I was. But unlike the partridge, I would never get across the open wheatfield, unseen. I scrambled back up the bank, and under the hedge, but not quickly enough. He had seen me. He ran, on his thin black legs like a bird. He caught up with me, grabbed my ankle, and hauled me backwards out through the blackthorn twigs.

'In trying to hide, you make your truancy all too obvious. Name? Your name, boy?'

I seemed to have lost my voice. I trembled. I shuffled uneasily. My hands were scratched. I tried to will myself away. I tried to pull up my shoulders, stand tall so that I might seem to be older, a farmboy returning from work. The rector was never fooled. He had the dark shiny eyes of a starling that swivelled slyly and saw everything. He would tell a boy's age even from a distance.

'Your name. What is your name?'

Why did the rector insist on hearing my name? He knew well enough who I was, or certainly ought to. Perhaps he enjoyed the power he gained by constantly asking one's name. Or perhaps the inhabitants of his parish really *did* look to him exactly the same, one totally indistinguishable from the next, just like the sheep of the fold that he constantly told us we were supposed to be.

His long strong fingers clutched hold of my shoulders like yellow claws, and without warning he shook me backwards and forwards, again and again.

The world in front of my eyes was quite dizzy from the shaking. The rector banged me on the side of the head with his Bible, first one side, then the other.

'Betts, sir.'

'Ah! So you can speak now? I met a boy called Betts in school today.'

'My brother Humphrey, sir. He is coming up the lane now, sir.'

'So there are two boys by the name of Betts?'

'There are three, sir.'

'And does the third Betts also truant?'

'No, sir. Pa says that he won't ever be able to go to school, sir.'

'And why not, may I ask? Does your father not know that according to the law he is obliged to send his sons regularly to school, or risk imprisonment of up to twenty-one days? Does he not know that schooling has been provided so that children may have a little learning, and become less dull than they mostly are?'

'Yes, sir.'

'Yes, sir? What do you mean by Yes, sir? Does your father wilfully keep your brother away from school?'

'My brother Jonas was born an idiot, sir.'

For once I felt grateful to Jonas. By talking about Jonas, the rector would forget about my misdeeds.

'Jonas Betts, aha yes. Unfortunate creature.' The rector rolled his eyes to the sky. 'May the Lord have mercy on him.'

Of course the rector knew who I was, who Jonas was. He

had refused to baptize Jonas, saying that a cretin had no soul and therefore no need of baptism. Ma had cried. Pa became so angry that in the end the rector had been forced to baptize Jonas, out of fear that Pa would knock him down.

'Betts, how old are you?'

'Nearly fourteen, sir,' I said, with a lowered voice, while pulling up my shoulders and standing tall.

'You are a liar, Betts.'

'Yes, sir.'

'Your father is a liar too. Evil runs in the blood. Gamekeepers tend, by nature of their work, towards cunning. You may tell him that if he does nothing to punish you for your deceit and truancy, I shall be forced to see to it myself.' I had once seen the rector punish a boy for blasphemy. I did not want to be punished by him.

'Remember, Betts, the eyes of the Lord are in every place. He can see even into your very heart.'

He finally released me, and made off on its black legs towards old Widow Craske's hovel.

Alice and Humphrey were hesitating a little way back. Now they quickly came to me. Alice gave me a hug.

'I'm sorry, Arthur. There was nothing we could do. He was in school all morning, checking on the register. He says Mr Pooley's been slacking and if attendances aren't kept up, he's to lose his pension. Oh, Arthur, I *do* wish you'd come to school more easily.'

I had been reluctant to leave home that morning. Now I was reluctant to return. But I had to get it over with.

I went straight round to the back of the shed. Pa was chopping wood.

'Pa, I have been truanting from school most days since Christmas. The rector says that you must hear of it, and that if you don't beat me, he will do so.'

After supper, as Pa buckled his leather belt round his waist, I heard Ma say, 'You beat him too hard, George. You had no reason to beat him like he was a dog.'

I felt like a dog as I crouched in the dark on the narrow stair and heard them through the wall. My thighs and backside were smarting with pain.

'I'm sorry, Elsie,' I heard Pa say. 'But he did wrong. And he knew it.'

Perhaps Pa knew that he had beaten me too hard. He did not say so, but he took a penny from the money jar in the cupboard and gave it to me to spend at the village store.

'But don't take to truanting nor poaching, Arthur. Go to school and learn your books. Then maybe you'll be a reader and a scholar and you won't have to labour all your life.'

I knew I could never be a scholar. Only one year younger than Alice, but a whole world away in achievement.

'Alice could make a fine scholar,' I said. 'She's the best in the school. Everybody knows it.'

Having Alice in his school was the best thing that had ever happened to Mr Pooley. She was like a bright beam in his hopeless task of educating the village, for he, like me, was trapped there.

Pa laughed. 'Alice'll go into service as soon as she can.'

'But she wants to train for the teaching. Mr Pooley wants to put her forward for the scholarship.'

'So I've heard.' Pa laughed again. 'Now don't go encouraging these high-faluting ideas in your sister's head!'

Even the thought of the warm penny in my hand, which would buy a string of liquorice, some aniseed, or better still a new piece of leather thong for my catapult, did not make the morning walk to school any less desolate. Alice tried to keep up my spirits with bright chat about the good things that lay ahead. A new hymn to learn, a story, geography when we heard from Mr Pooley about his long ago visit to Heidelberg, Würzburg, and Tübingen.

I had no interest in faraway places. The places I wanted to know about were all around us.

Alice's profitable days at school were fast running out

while mine stretched miserably, drearily ahead forever. I couldn't leave until I was fourteen, or had passed my Standard 6, whichever came first. The bell on the school roof stopped. I knew there was no chance that I would ever pass Standard 6. I would have to wait till age alone caught up with me.

Mr Pooley, standing on the raised dais, greeted me kindly. He was thin and anaemic. Alice said this was because he had no mother or wife to care for him. He smiled as I slouched in and patted my arm.

'Good to see you, Arthur.' I knew he knew about the beating and was sorry. But there was no way he could understand that I suffered not from Pa's beating, but from the stifling in my head as I entered the bleak and sunless building. For Alice's sake, he was prepared to like me. For Alice's sake, I would try to endure a day's schooling.

The noise that morning was intolerable. One of the infants wailed incessantly for its mother. The older girls recited their rules of grammar in monotonous waves of chanting like church prayers. Three big boys chattered, played dice under cover of their slates, and clattered their boots on the floor to cover the rattle of dice. They were marking time till they could leave at the end of the summer.

Mr Pooley rang the handbell on his desk and ordered us to continue in silence.

'The Inspector will be coming *at any time* to test our Standards,' he said with a faint sigh. 'Last year, only three from the entire school reached the correct level of attainment for their age. The Governors were not pleased.'

Mr Pooley received six shillings and sixpence for every pass. It had been a lean year. Now the Governors threatened to take away his attendance allowance.

The crying infant continued to wail, as unaware as ever of what a school was supposed to be for. Mr Pooley told the child's elder brother to take him home, and the rest of us to continue writing our spelling words as he dictated them.

'Deuteronomy.' I knew it was in the Bible, but not how to write it.

'Constitution.' I did not know what that meant, let alone the letters used to form the word.

I spat on my slate, rubbed it clean with my sleeve and tried again. But what was the use? There was no reason why they would come out any righter this time than the last, or the time before that.

I stared up at the windows, set in a row, high in the wall so that no one could see the trees, or the fields, or the earth, only a patch of sky, blue and bright, which urged me to be out there. I looked across the hall at Alice, her head bent industriously over her copybook. She looked content, fulfilled, as she glanced up once to help a younger child pronounce some word. During the day, there was a brief time of happiness when Alice was called to the front to read aloud to the school. She told the story clearly and thoughtfully. It was more like hearing a speaking voice than a reading one. And briefly, I was transfixed by the tale of two adventurers who climbed the jagged mountains of Switzerland in search of rare flowers. Briefly, I too wanted to be able to do the same as Alice, to take hold of stories in books as only a reader can.

But all too soon, the view of mountains, the thrill of great heights, the first sight of rare blue gentians nestling in a rocky crevice was over and we were back at the dull classroom slog again.

'How many furlongs, rods, yards, feet, inches and barley corns, will reach round the Earth, supposing it, according to the best calculations, to be 25,020 miles?' Mr Pooley intoned, as he wrote up the arithmetic question in his elegant script on the black board. I kept the question in my head since I couldn't read it. But there was no way I could think of working it out.

Up at the window, I saw a butterfly trapped inside the pane. All morning, it tried to batter its way through the glass with its dark velvet wings. During the mid-morning recess, I climbed onto the bench, then onto the top of the cupboard, and from there, onto the windowledge to set the butterfly free.

I looked through the dusty pane and faraway in the distance saw the twist of smoke curling up through the trees at Pit Bottom. Pa had lit the fire. Ma would soon be putting on the evening meal to cook. Little Jenny must be scampering about the kitchen getting under Ma's feet, and Jonas lying quiet. If Jonas only knew how fortunate he was.

Three more hours.

'Arthur! Please come down from there at once.' Mr Pooley ordered me down from the ledge before I had time to catch the tortoiseshell. The whole school was to learn Psalm One Hundred, *O be Joyful Unto the Lord*, by heart before the rector's visit in the afternoon.

It was not the rector who came, but his wife. That was one thing to be grateful for. She was not fierce like a starling, but small and dithery like a hedge sparrow. The big boys at the back ignored her.

'The recitation, children,' said Mr Pooley, and we shuffled to our feet.

Led by the voice of Alice, and one other named Bessie Godfrey, who had also managed to learn the psalm, we somehow mumbled our way through the 24 verses. It sounded like the bleating of thirty-seven lost sheep. The rector's wife smiled throughout, as though listening to music.

'Well done. That was *very* good, children,' she said. Did she not know that she was lying?

Mr Pooley rubbed his thin hands together and offered her a chair. Perhaps he would not lose his attendance allowance after all. Perhaps the two shillings needlework grant would be increased to three shillings?

The rector's wife did not sit down, but hopped up and

down between the rows of benches as she began our Religious Knowledge.

'All you young people in this school are the sons and daughters of labourers,' she began, and smiled round at us.

Bessie Godfrey, a big girl, whose parents ran the village store, twitched in her place and tossed one of her plaits over her shoulder so that it flicked the child sitting behind her. She was no labourer's child. 'And as the rector explained last week, our Creator has chosen where each of us shall be in this life. He placed each of us where we are, whether high or low, He gave us the role we now have in society.' She took up Mr Pooley's chalk and wrote a list on the blackboard.

'Now who's going to read this for me?'

My heart pounded. She must not pick on me. I shrank below the level of Bessie in front. I closed my eyes so as not to catch hers.

'You, dear. Yes, you.' The rector's wife pointed, of course, to Alice. Alice stood up, straightened her apron, folded her hands behind her back and read in her lovely voice.

'Duty towards your Neighbour: Number One: Girls and boys must never pick or steal. Number Two: Girls and boys must never lie nor have any envy of folk better or luckier than themselves. Number three: Girls and boys must learn to labour truly to get their own living.'

I didn't listen to the rector's wife's list, only to the sound of those soft syllables, like a dove cooing.

'Number Ten: Boys and girls must order themselves lowly and reverently to their betters.'

Alice sat down, blushing faintly.

'Thank you,' said the rector's wife. 'A fine young reader. Those of you who can will copy the list into your books.'

When school was over, I climbed back up to the window ledge to set the butterfly free. But it was dead. A spider was laboriously wrapping its soft auburn-spotted wings in a shroud of web, in readiness to eat it.

Chapter 5

*P*A still had no work.

'I'll take in laundry,' said Ma.

For sixpence a bundle, she did other people's dirty washing as well as our own. Some of her customers could afford it little better than we could. They paid, not so much for clean linen on Friday, as to savour the grandeur of Ma and Alice arriving at their back doors to collect and deliver. The bending and straining over the wash-board was not good for Ma. Humphrey and I helped with the wringing, taking one end each of a steaming sheet and twisting with all our might. Some pieces of wet laundry were so heavy that, often as not, we would drop them and have to rinse and wring all over again.

But for the little ones, life at Pit Bottom went on much as it always had done. Little Jenny had enough to eat. She had our Ma's skirt within sight to cling to. She was happy to potter all day. Jonas was too dim to know where he was, let alone understand that a shameful lowering in our status had taken place.

Indeed, Jonas was probably better off than before. Since Pa no longer had to devote every waking hour to tending the pheasant chicks, or touring the copses and spinneys, he could go about his business of looking for work with Jonas in his arms.

Jonas had always been weak. He hadn't learned to walk, nor to talk, although he grunted and grizzled a great deal. I'd seen him smile too when I waved a striped pigeon feather in front of his eyes, though nobody believed me.

Pa now had the time to build a small wooden box-bed in which Jonas could sit, propped up, so that he could see activity going on around, and feel that he was in the centre of life. At night, Jonas slept in this box by the grate and benefitted from the remains of the heat. His thin, twig-like limbs held the cold more than ours did.

Perhaps Mr Wilkins had been right when he said that children and game cannot be successfully reared in the same pen. I didn't care too much how the game birds were faring with their new bachelor keeper. But Jonas was certainly flourishing. He even had a spot of colour in his cheeks.

The hot summer, forecast by the early briar rose which Pa had found, seemed to go on forever. The good weather lasted after we had finished school. Even the rector could not make children stay away from hay-making. But the long hot days did not help our vegetables.

The cabbage seedlings all failed.

'Them seeds were in too late,' said Pa, prodding at the crumbly earth with the toe of his boot. 'Soil were too dry.'

No sooner did each small shoot appear, than it shrivelled in the sun and died for want of moisture. But the main crop potatoes were growing up good and busy. Humphrey and I helped Pa earth up the roots so that the tubers wouldn't green.

Every day, every week, Pa tried for labouring work. He had no success. He was promised one day's swede-trimming later on, and a few days road-making, depending on the weather, in the autumn. But no farmer would give him harvest work when the labour of children was cheap.

'I could move,' I heard him say to Ma. 'Up Lincolnshire. They say there's plenty potato-pulling up there.'

But Ma didn't care for the thought of Pa going away to live among strangers.

In other parts of the country there was plenty of work for women and children too, or so we believed. There was stone-picking for a penny a day, or lace-making. But Pa would have none of it.

'No son of *mine*'ll break his back for a penny a day. Nor lace-making. Turn a girl blind before she's twenty?'

Even bird-scaring, so Pa said, was to send a boy deaf from the constant clatter of the rattle he had to shake.

In late summer, Pa began to prepare, like the good provider that Ma said he was, for winter.

'Never seen so many berries,' he said, nodding his head at the dark clusters on the hawthorn bush. 'Going to be a hard one.'

The sun beat down. The ripening cornfield shimmered in the heat. The earth was hard-baked like rock. The level in the rain-water tub dropped down and down, nearly to the bottom, so that one week Ma even had to buy water from the water-carrier so that she would not lose custom by being unable to return her customers' clean linen. It seemed impossible that there could ever be winter.

Only I knew of Pa's preparations, and I was astounded. It was like the business of lying. Although the rector had warned me not to lie, his wife could. Although I was to be law-abiding, Pa was not.

On a dry evening, Pa took a net and went up into the barley field where the partridges were jugging. As though to atone for the heavy beating, he let me follow so long as I watched in silence and did not ask questions.

First, he listened for the partridges calling each other up for roosting time, so he would know where they were laying up. They slept in barley-stubble or dry grass. We went along quietly and drew the net against the wind. It was more than twenty yards long and a good ten feet wide, with a close mesh. It was heavy for me to pull and he certainly couldn't have done it without my help. We kept the upper part clear of the ground, and the hind part dragged low over the stubble. There was no difficulty in catching birds. We could hear them fluttering underneath. It was still the close season.

They hadn't learned to be wary of banging guns, and crashing about of the shooting party. We could almost pick them up off the ground as we walked, except that they were not ours to pick. They were his lordship's to shoot.

'What'll you do with them?'

'There's a man,' Pa grunted.

I knew who the man was. It would have to be Joseph Plumb.

Pa grunted. 'Could be'.

Joseph Plumb's official business was mole-catcher. This gave him reason to be anywhere, wherever he needed to be for his other occupations. He moved from village to village, and back again, and no one ever knew where he lived. He was never caught with anything more than a couple of dead moles on him.

Pa wrung the birds' necks. When they were dead, he lovingly stroked their soft plumage. Then he tucked them inside his jacket. The net was bundled up tight and hidden under brambles.

'What man?'

'Stop them questions. A dishonest man of course. Sells them to a poulterer in Reepham Market.'

'What'll you get?'

'Half a crown. Though I daresay he'll sell 'em for more than double that.' He listened to the tick-tick of birds still feeding in the field. 'A brace of them is worth more than gold dust up London right now.'

I had never eaten partridge. 'Are they good?'

'It's not the taste they're after. They've a nasty peckish sort of taste if you ask me. It's the sight of them, plump and roasted on the dining-table on the twelfth. That's what they're after. Claim to have shot them themselves. Won't know they weren't even shot, just picked. Some folks are daft.'

The next day, I saw Pa slip two silver sixpences into the money-jar in the kitchen cupboard. It was far less than he was expecting, only a quarter of the market value of the birds.

'Why didn't you ask for the half a crown, like you said?'

'I wasn't in no position to bargain, was I now?' he muttered. 'Man with the blood in his pocket is always guilty. And don't you go talking to your Ma! What she don't know about won't upset her!'

The money-jar was kept regularly topped up, though nobody except me, knew how. Ma never saw Pa slip in the extra coins, though several times she was pleasantly confused when she went to the jar for twopence for a quart of milk, or a penny for a pinch of mustard powder, to find, mysteriously, more than she had remembered putting by from the washing. But then he had to lay off the partridges for a while. Wilkins was on the look-out, for he had noticed the number in each covey dwindling rapidly.

I was surprised at my Pa turning from keeper to poacher in so short a time. I feared that it was just like the rector warned. The evil in our blood was beginning to show. And I was even more astonished by his bitterness. It was as though, all summer long, when he had appeared to be cheerfully busying himself with the garden, and playing with the little ones in the sun, his anger had been heated up and simmering away under the apparent good humour. I had not realized the shame he felt at bringing no money into the family, while our Ma, washing and wringing till her hands were red and raw, at least earned a shilling or two a week.

Pa held up a leveret he had snared early one morning. It was still warm, and its young fur was pale and silky.

'See that?' said Pa. 'His lordship's! And where do I get it? In the wood behind. And whose wood is that? His lordship's woods. And Great Wood, where I picked that long-tail. Whose is that? And Makin's Farm?'

Everywhere, as far as one could travel in a day, appeared to belong to his lordship.

'That's right. And so it all does.'

His lordship, it seemed to me, must be like God. Both ruled our lives and owned our world, yet I had never seen either. I had to take other people's word for it that they existed.

'You climb to the top of the church tower, Arthur, everything you see from up there – and you can see more than twenty miles round when the weather's right – belongs to his lordship.'

'God made the world, didn't he?'

'Could be,' said my Pa.

'The rector said so. Why did he give so much of it to his lordship, and so little to the others?'

'You ask too many questions. It's not God's fault. It's man's. You remember Adam and Eve brought sin into the world? We're all of us guilty. His lordship is guilty. Mr Wilkins is guilty. The farmers. Keepers poaching off the land. The magistrate – and if I should be caught, pray God Almighty I won't – is guilty. All guilty!' He shook his fist at me. 'But who's the most guilty? Answer me that.'

I had no idea.

'I am!' Pa roared, so loud I thought someone might hear us. 'With seven mouths to feed.' He waved his arms about dropping his sack. 'And how do you think I'm to feed you lot through winter?'

Pa shouted at the trees as though addressing Adam and all the ranks of guilty men. I wondered if, not only was the evil rising in his blood, but if he was going mad, like the old woman who had lived in Pit Bottom cottage before us.

I wanted to ask Alice about the causes of madness. But then I would have to tell her of Pa's unaccountable fits of anger when out snaring, and I was sworn to secrecy.

Pa killed his victims quickly and cleanly. I went with him when he toured the snares to collect up his victims or, if there were none, to remove the snares and hide them if a keeper was expected that way. After he had loosened the wire round a dead rabbit's neck, he spoke softly to the corpse, and would gently stroke the long soft ears before tying the hind legs together with a piece of twine, and looping the twine through his belt so that the animal was hidden under his coat.

If it was not dead, he would break its neck across his knee.

'Quick, quiet and steady, that's the way. No rush.' While Pa worked he muttered to himself.

When he had half a dozen rabbits, he set off along the footpath to the next village to dispose of them. He never gave them or sold them to any person in our village, and we never ate rabbit-pie or game soup at home. We ate what was bought with the money, fat pork, flour, sometimes a bit of treacle or sugar.

One evening when we reached the snare, we found only torn white fluff, blood and bones. The fox had been there before us. Pa quickly cleared away the giveaway traces, and buried the disembodied hind legs in ground-cover, for wherever a fox had been, Wilkins or one of his men was sure to come soon after.

But it was Jo Plumb who discovered us first. He had been crouching behind a screen of bracken watching us for several minutes before I realized he was there. I nudged my Pa.

From behind his cover, Jo Plumb hissed and spat, then slunk over towards my Pa, moving low to the ground with his little pink ferrety eyes glancing this way and that. He wore layer upon layer of ragged garments, filthy old coats, the colour of leaf-mould, and he blended easily into the background of hedge or grass. His brown felt hat was stained with bird droppings to mark the hours he had sat quietly waiting beneath a roosters' tree.

He beckoned my Pa to follow him and they stood under a tree for a moment.

I heard no words exchanged between them but some kind

of deal seemed to have been done. Another shilling could go into the money-jar.

Since Pa had taken me into his confidence, I supposed that he wanted me to work as his accomplice. I too would help keep the jar filled so that I too could enjoy Ma's confusion and surprise.

Early one morning, I took one of the copper snares from the shed and hurried away to a thicket a mile or so from home. I was getting to know the ways of the hare by now. I chose a well-used run where fresh droppings showed it had been used earlier. I stopped up the hare's other runs so he would be sure to come along mine. I rubbed my hands along them and spat on them, then he wouldn't pass by my scent. Now he would be sure to come along the run I had chosen.

I set the snare as I had seen Pa do, just ahead of a pair of paw-marks on the run so his head would go through. I set it not too high or it would catch his front paws, nor too low or it would take his hind paws. I scattered a handful of leaves and leaf mould to cover signs of my meddling. Then I ran off and lay down in a nearby ditch to wait. I dozed in the ditch but I didn't have to wait more than an hour. I heard a quick squeal and knew the wire had hanged him.

Before Pa went out on his evening walk, I showed him my catch. The intimacy which I thought had grown between us was instantly gone.

'You will never do that again!' he said in a low and frightening tone.

In my pride at having trapped the hare with so little trouble, I had not bothered to notice that the animal, though hanged, was still breathing, its faint heart still beating. Through all the day hours since I first trapped it and hid it in the shed to show to Pa, it had been lying there, half alive.

Pa broke its neck. Then he took off his belt, pulled down my trousers, right there in the garden behind the cottage, and strapped me harder than he had strapped me for the truanting.

Then, he turned and walked away without a word. I ran back up to the Small Wood and hid myself in the leaves and wept, not for the stinging on my skin, not for the suffering I had caused the hare, but for the hurt I had done to my Pa. I knew that I had failed him.

We did not light the fire till late in the afternoon to save fuel, except Friday when Ma did her weekly baking. All day, the kitchen was filled with the sweet yeasty smell of fresh bread and crusty pie. But once it was done, Ma didn't stay indoors to enjoy it. Early on Friday evenings, she and Alice set off for the village to return clean linen and collect dirty.

Despite the demeanour of the task, trudging from door to door with the heavy basket on her arm which never grew lighter but whose contents merely changed from sweet-smelling and newly laundered to soiled and stinking, she looked forward to her trip.

'My head in and out of that hot oven all morning and I'm more than glad to get out and about and see a few friendly faces!' She tied on her bonnet and took up her basket. Alice took Jenny and Humphrey by the hand. They went too, cleaned up as though for church.

'Have to set a good example, and show the world we're not destitute.'

The moment Ma was gone, Pa set to work. He had two ounces of gunpowder from a man who worked at the powder mill, in exchange for one rabbit.

'Green India,' he said, opening the twist of blue paper. 'Never seen anything like it before.' It was coarse and grainy, more like sand than powder. They used Green India for blasting at the quarry.

Pa was going to fill his empty cartridges. Now that the season had begun, it would be possible for him to take out his shotgun. The report would be more easily mistaken for someone else's legal shot.

I shifted Jonas in his wooden box out of the way. He had had his turn of being by the fire all day. I pulled up a stool.

Now it was my turn, and I wanted to see what Pa was doing. He cut wads for the cartridges from felt. The powder was in an old copper powder flask. He used it, and the lead shot, sparingly, for they were not cheap to buy.

Once they were filled and closed, Pa put the cartridges carefully into the bread-oven, to use the remains of the heat for drying them out.

'Never throw them down, Arthur,' Pa said, as he took up an empty cartridge case. 'Neither keeper nor poacher ever throws a spent cartridge down on the ground. You pick it up and put it in your pocket.'

The kitchen was quiet, only the sound of ash falling into the grate. It was the same still quiet as on the night that the mouchers came. I watched, remembering not to speak or ask my questions. That was how he liked it.

'Only gentry can afford to throw them down. If the keeper throws them down, it gives away his whereabouts, exact. And same for him who's no right to be there.'

I knew, from collecting gentry's empty cartridges, that you could tell from the lingering smell of spent powder, how long since it was fired.

Pa laid the filled tubes gently, side by side, not touching, on the warm floor of the oven.

'Don't forget that now, Arthur. Treat the powder like it was a baby asleep. Gently, with respect.'

It was the last sensible thing he said.

Maybe the quarry-worker's powder was too dry, or too coarse, or maybe Pa packed it too tightly, or too loosely so that it shifted about too freely inside the waxed cardboard. Or maybe he was hurrying to be done before Ma came back.

Whatever the cause, as he tapped on the brass cap of the last cartridge, gentle soft taps more like pats than blows, the cartridge exploded.

I didn't hear the noise, only saw the white flash which threw me backwards off my stool and down onto the stone flags where I lay for a second or two, or maybe a minute or two, or maybe an hour. It was dark when I came to and the smell of Friday's cooked pie hung in the air, mingling with the sulphurous smell of gunpowder.

I staggered to my feet. Pa too had been thrown backwards by the blast, right across the kitchen. He was slumped against the wall with his eyes wide open, staring, and a small piece at the side of his head was blown clean away.

Chapter 6

*I*T took the strength of all five of us, myself, Ma, Alice and Humphrey as well as little Jenny who grappled with his great legs, to carry Pa up the narrow stairway to the loft. We heaved him onto the wooden bed. Ma unbuttoned his gaiters, unlaced his boots, and covered him with a blanket. His hands were as cold as ice, but his pale blue eyes stared open, and seemed to watch us as we bustled around in panic.

The explosion had chipped away a piece of his skull so that you could see his brains showing through. At least, Humphrey said you could see his brains. It looked more like a dark clotted mass of sheep's intestines to me. There was a slow flow of blood down his forehead.

Ma sent Alice downstairs to fill a stone bottle with hot water to put at Pa's feet. She sent Jenny to fetch another blanket, Humphrey to find clean cloth in the kitchen press, and me out into the garden to fetch a bunch of cobwebs.

'Quickly! Don't just stand there gawping! Before he bleeds to death!'

He did not look to me as though he was bleeding to death. I had once seen a pig bleed to death. There was more blood, and more shrieking and more kicking than now. Pa just lay, his head on a cushion, staring. But if Ma said he was bleeding to death, then I would obey. I hurtled down the steps, colliding with Jenny coming up with the extra blanket, across the kitchen, and up to the thicket at the end of the garden. A great dark holly bush, almost a tree, grew in the middle of the thicket. Its upper branches were already heavy with winter berries, but they were still green, like peas in a pod. Its dusty lower branches, sheltered from rain and wind, were festooned with cobwebs, old ones and new.

I crawled in under the prickles to gather them.

The fresh ones stuck to my skin and disintegrated, and the old grey ones drifted away and had to be re-caught. I gathered handfuls scratching my hands and wrists. But I would save his life. I would save his precious blood from flowing.

I ran indoors with my grey bouquet and Ma applied them to Pa's wound to staunch the flow. But head wounds don't bleed. It had stopped of its own accord. There was now only a trickle.

Alice set the kitchen to rights, putting back the chairs in their places quickly and quietly, and wiping the scorch mark off the ceiling. As she swept the floor, she found the chip of bone and showed it to me. We washed it and put it in a cup on the mantlepiece. But she didn't tell Ma.

I cleared away all traces of the cartridges before Jenny or Humphrey should come and fiddle with them. I took Pa's gun from where it was leaning in the corner and carefully finished cleaning it with the piece of rag and paraffin oil, as he had been doing. Then I wrapped it in the old sack, and put it back under the eaves.

All that night and the next day Pa lay in bed, speechless, witless, but apparently in no pain. We didn't know if he could hear us or not. We crept about, hardly speaking above whispers, not rattling cups, or scraping chair legs, not turning over in bed, shushing Jenny and Jonas if ever they cried, as though we believed that our quietness could somehow save him. This was our only means of trying to help.

Ma did not summon the doctor. She was afraid that he would be suspicious about the nature of Pa's accident. Then people on the estate would also become suspicious. Then Pa would be arrested and sent to gaol.

'How could they arrest him like this, when he can't even stand up?' said Alice.

'When he's recovered,' said Ma. 'Just like they did for your father's Uncle Robert.'

Alice began to rattle about with the iron pans on the fire. Ma went upstairs again to Pa. I asked Alice,

'What Uncle Robert?'

'Sssh,' said Alice, and busied herself with cutting the black eyes out of the potatoes.

'*Tell* me,' I ordered her. I had never heard of anything of any uncle of Pa's.

Alice was evasive. 'It was a long time back. They don't talk of it. Maybe even before Pa was born. It's not important.'

'It is. Tell me. If it wasn't important why did Ma mention it now? What happened?'

Without looking at me, Alice said, 'Transportation. He had fourteen years. He never came back.'

Pa began to recover. He sat up and let Ma feed him a bowlful of gruel. Then he worsened.

Altogether Pa took eight days to die. For eight nights Ma slept upright on a chair at his side. The doctor had to be called in at the end anyway, not to cure Pa but to certify his death, to verify that Pa had injured himself falling down the stairs.

The doctor came halfway up the lane in his gig but the wheels stuck in the ruts like wheels always do, so he had to walk the last hundred yards of the way and got his suede boots all dusty. He seemed content to accept our explanation for the manner of Pa's death. Certainly the stairs were steep enough and dark enough to cause an accident if you should slip.

The doctor had done nothing for Pa, but he charged a guinea for his visit and another ten shillings for writing out the certificate.

Ma paid him out of the money-jar.

'He's done nothing to earn it,' Alice muttered, 'except wear a fancy silk hat.'

The doctor said, 'Thank you,' and 'I offer you my condolences,' put on his hat, and stepped briskly out of the house and down the path, as though unwilling to be contaminated by our breath a moment longer than he had to.

'Humphrey!' said our Ma. 'You'll go and fetch Mrs Craske right away.'

'No, please, Ma, not me!'

Once, in a neighbourly act, Ma had sent him down to her hovel with a jar of apple curd. Ma received no thanks for it, let alone a return gesture. Humphrey had come back more frightened of her than ever.

'It's the way she smiles,' he said.

I had only seen a brief glimpse of her beaky face through a window, and a far-off sight of her bent back as she scurried down to assist some recently dead, or newborn, member of the village.

'I'll go with him,' I said. I wanted to see her close to.

I rapped sternly at her door, like the doctor had knocked at ours. She opened instantly as though expecting our call.

She was not old, probably no older than our own Ma, but she was not clean. She pulled a woolly shawl, stained with spills, round her shoulders with dirty fingers.

Before I even had time to explain the reason for my call, she said, 'So she wants me for the laying-out does she? Tell her I'll be up directly.' Then I saw the smile.

She had no teeth in the top half of her mouth, and the bottom ones were brown. Humphrey was right. It was better if she didn't smile.

Within fifteen minutes, Mrs Craske was there, filling our own kitchen with her dark authority, ordering Alice for a bucket of fresh water, ordering me for strips of sheeting, Humphrey to find a clean night-shirt.

While she carried out her task upstairs, I sat in the garden and ate a bright sharp crab apple. I felt proud to think that

Mrs Craske, usually busy elsewhere, had come to this house. Now our house was the centre of interest, the newspoint. There was always something important about having a death in the family.

Pa looked better dead. Mrs Craske had combed his yellow hair across the side of his head so that the hole didn't show. And though his hands, resting on his chest, were now even colder and paler than before, there were not his staring empty eyes to cope with. Mrs Craske had closed them so that he seemed almost asleep, except that he never slept flat on his back.

Ma made each of us go up and kiss him goodbye, even Jonas who wriggled and struggled when held up to his Pa's lifeless lips. I did not know where Ma thought Pa was going to, apart from into the hole already dug, for five shillings, in the churchyard.

The two men who had dug it came up from the village with the bier. They had difficulty manoeuvring the coffin up the narrow stairs, and even more difficulty getting it down again. They muttered to each other on the dark corner halfway down.

They lifted it up onto the bier standing in the garden, and pushed it down the bumpy lane with us following behind. The coffin began to slide sideways, just as the pots and pans had slid off the handcart on that first journey. Humphrey and I walked alongside it, holding it. It was not oak, only elm, and had no brass fittings, just our Pa's name written on with black ink. Nonetheless, I felt important.

None of us cried. There didn't seem much point.

'Except to satisfy *them*,' said Alice bitterly. A cluster of villagers had gathered round the church gate to watch us process into the church and then out again for the burial. Alice did not enjoy being the centre of attention as I did.

As we straggled home up the lane, not watched by anyone, Ma said, with a kind of satisfaction, 'At least he wasn't buried on the parish.'

She had gained some strange comfort from having been able to pay for the funeral all out of the money-jar.

The coffin had cost five pounds. Then there were the gravediggers, and payment to the rector for conducting the service. Of all of them, only Mrs Craske refused to accept her fee. Ma stopped by at her hovel on our way home from the funeral.

'I'll collect payment when I call again about the other matter,' she said, showing her bare brown gums in a horrid smile, and nodding her head.

'What other matter? Why is she coming again?' I asked.

'Ma's new baby,' said Alice. 'You know all about it.'

But I didn't know. Alice knew everything about everything, while I knew nothing about nothing. 'Before Christmas. Soon. Mrs Craske knows we'll have to call on her then. She knows Ma's got no money left now, not after paying all that lot out. Perhaps she thinks we'll have more by next month. Goodness knows how.'

I glanced at Ma ahead of us in the lane, Jonas in her arms, Jenny tagging along with a hand on her skirt, and now another young one growing beneath her skirt, already pushing its bulk against the gathered tucks. How could we possibly house and care for another child? Pa had died leaving Ma nothing but his gun hidden from her under the thatch, and a chip of his head hidden from her in a cup. All the money he had been saving for her in the money-jar had gone to pay for his own funeral, without Ma even knowing.

Immediately after the funeral, Ma went up to the loft without having a cup of tea and slept through for two days and nights without waking.

'We shouldn't let her sleep on and on,' I said. 'It's not natural. She might sleep herself to death.'

Pa's body had gone but death still seemed to linger in that gloomy space under the thatch. 'Then there'd be nobody for us.'

The glamour of a death in the family had worn off.

'No, we must let her alone,' said Alice. 'Sleep's the best thing for her. She's tired out from nursing Pa, and there's the new one growing, eating up all the goodness in her.'

The same night, after Ma had fallen into her deep sleep, Mrs Craske, for all her apparent unneighbourliness, brought us up a hot jam roly-poly tied in muslin cloth. She did not stay, or even come in. She pushed the pudding to Alice over the threshold.

'And I'll have the muslin back, and washed, directly,' she said.

I made up the fire. Humphrey drew up the stools. Alice shared out the suet and jam. We sat round in the red glow, eating the roly-poly from dishes balanced on our laps. Then we drank warmed milk and Alice read aloud to us some poems while Humphrey and I fed Jonas, taking it in turns to press the morsels into his mouth with our fingers, and making his jaws chew, and his throat swallow. What he spat out we pushed back in again.

'From now on, we must all be very very good, and all work very hard to help keep Mother happy,' said Alice solemnly, as she closed her book. We nodded in agreement. I knew what I should do.

Even though it was the night of Pa's funeral, for a moment, in that close warm circle of two sisters and two brothers, I felt an uncanny kind of joy.

Chapter 7

WE'LL *not* go gleaning!' said Ma, petulant like Jenny in a rage. 'Do you hear me, Alice? I am mistress of this house and I won't have it.'

Ma was proud. She had never had to send us gleaning before.

'But Ma, we *have* to go,' Alice pleaded.

Our sack of meal was sagging limp against the kitchen wall. We had to have a full sack to see us through the winter.

'In Scotland,' said Humphrey, 'they eat oats in winter, like horses. But they're all savages up there.'

Ma was obstinate about the gleaning. Alice kept quite calm but absolutely resolute.

'We'll glean. I shall go, and Arthur, and the little ones. You needn't come, Ma. In your condition, you shouldn't anyway.'

'Very well,' said our Ma with a deep sigh. 'I won't hide my face away, as though I'm ashamed of anything.'

We watched the weather as keenly as those to whom the harvest belonged. Some years, there would be a good hot week for harvesting and then, come gleaning day, the weather would break and the skies open up. The fields would become a mudbath, and gleaners were drenched and shivering. The damp wheat they gathered would rot in their bags. But for us, the weather held.

We were up before sunrise when the sky was still dark blue, just becoming streaked with faint yellow on the horizon.

Ma dressed in her best bonnet with a piece of black satin ribbon in a rosette stitched to the side, on account of Pa. She wore her best floral shawl, and the silver trinket round her neck.

'Ma, you can't –!' Alice started to say. Nobody ever went gleaning in their best. But Ma told us all to change into our best too, with boots well blackened, hair damped and combed. The girls wore newly starched aprons, and Jonas was in a clean smock.

I didn't mind having to glean. I almost looked forward to it. But I was perplexed by this business of dressing up. Ma spent half her life pounding our clothes on the washboard, and trying to whiten our linen with wood ash. Yet now she was sending us out to do dusty, earthy field-work in those same whitened garments. All her washing labour would be wasted within half an hour. Besides, I feared the boys in the village might laugh if they saw me.

Alice told me to be quiet and stop complaining. 'Don't you see the ordeal for *her*, going down to the village, newly widowed? She's afraid the people'll give her pity. The least we can do is show our support.'

My jacket was tight under the arms, and the stiff collar rubbed my neck. But since it was not yet day-break, nobody saw us. Alice carried the lunch basket with a can of cold tea and a loaf made from the stale flour dust at the bottom of our sack, and Humphrey and I took turns to carry Jonas. He was too heavy now for Ma.

We made our way in the morning twilight, down Pit Bottom Lane, between the open fields. There was a strange stillness in the air, as though something astounding was about to happen. Every time I was up at this hour, I sensed the same mixture of thrill and fear. Then the tip of the new sun jerked its way over the top of a distant hedgerow, and golden light flooded across the land. The world had begun again. And looking at the stretch of hedge beside the plough, the oak trees catching the sun on their upper leaves and dark shadows underneath, the brilliant colour of the grass, I was overcome with the certainty that it was all mine. I owned all I could see.

'No, Arthur!' said Alice. 'You mustn't *say* those things. It's his lordship's land and you know it.'

'No, I don't mean owning for a lifetime. I mean something more than that, beyond that. Owning forever.'

'His lordship doesn't own it just for a lifetime either. When his lordship dies, it'll go on to his son, and then his son after that, forever and ever. "Thou shalt not covet." You can't have it.'

Alice never did understand what I was trying to say. Or else I just hadn't the right words for it.

'It's like stealing,' said Alice. 'Wanting something that's someone else's.'

'You can't steal just by looking,' I said, 'and I'm going to go on looking.' I took Jonas from Humphrey for my turn.

When we reached the opening of the gleaning field, there was already a little queue forming, and a farmhand at the gate keeping guard. Nobody was allowed onto the stubble before five o'clock. Widows and the poorest of the poor were admitted first. There were several lone women, widows, or spinsters with no one to earn for them, though Mrs Craske was not among them, and a family of orphans who were being brought up by their aunt. Our arrival at the back of the short queue caused a stir. It might have been our well-turned out appearance or, more likely, the revelation that we were reduced to their level of poverty. Some people had assumed that our Ma, with her hoity-toity respectable ways, must have a little something tucked away.

The rays of sun leaped through the trees now and spread in striped bands across the field. We laid out our sheet flat on the ground, with a stone at each corner to hold it down. Then we raced out onto the stubble, and headed for a profitable stretch on the curve of the field where the waggon, turning, would always spill a little.

Ma did not glean. She was too large now to bend. She sat on a bale of straw with Jonas, guarding our hoard and giving us little nods of encouragement each time we ran back to her and emptied our bags on to the spread cloth.

Up and down between the spiky rows the three of us toiled, gathering in the single grains, the ears, and sometimes, when lucky, a whole handful of stalks which the reapers had missed or dropped. The sun rose higher. They day grew hotter. The girls tied on their sun bonnets. I felt I would faint from the heat. I could tell, from glancing up at Humphrey's glowing beetroot face beside me, that mine was the same.

At last, Ma allowed us to take off our jackets and hang them on a hedge. We had made our good impression.

The field was full now, the late arrivals having to glean in the dip where it was mostly thistles. Nobody noticed or cared who was who. I stood up and stretched my aching back and gazed at them spread right across the field, stooping, pecking their way up and down the rows of stubble like large pheasants.

Till midday it was easy to work optimistically. Then the sharp pieces of chaff worked their way into my boots, and rubbed against the skin with every step. The stubble grazed my hands. The dry dust got into my eyes. My back ached from being bent double hour after hour.

Our gleanings were ground for us by the miller.

'And he'll doubtless take a bit for himself from the top of the bag,' said Alice.

But at least he charged us nothing and delivered the sack of flour right to the door, carrying it on his back up the last rutted part of the lane where his cart could not go.

'Lovely bit of leazings you got in there, Mrs Betts,' he said, patting the sack approvingly as he sat down in the biggest chair.

Labourers who had gleaned a great deal left their sack sitting in the kitchen for a week or more, to be admired by passers-by. But nobody passed by our home, though ours was a fine sack, well worth the viewing.

So it sat there and occupied the chair. It was too heavy to move and we had to edge respectfully round when we needed to get past. It was fat and white, its floury belly bulged over the seat, and in the evening it seemed to leer at me. Suddenly, I couldn't stand the sight of it any more.

That was our Pa's chair. He hadn't been fat and leering. I would rather have had him sitting there than the fullest bag of gleanings in the world. I punched it with my fist, then kicked it. It toppled to the floor and I kicked it some more. I went on kicking till the twine at the top came undone. The flour spilled out onto the stone floor in a torrent. Only Alice was in the kitchen to see me, and Jonas who never saw or said anything. I stopped kicking and watched the flour flow like water. Then I began to cry.

'You haven't spilled very much,' Alice said quietly. 'Only a little. We can save most of it.'

'It's spoiled. It's dirty. We can't eat dirt off the floor.'

But she swept it up carefully, trying to sort the soiled flour from the clean. 'Never mind, Arthur.'

'I'll make it up,' I said. 'I promise.'

'I'll make a nice crusty pastry and nobody'll know about the dirt if we don't tell. Go and fetch some blackberries with Jenny.'

I took a basin and Jenny's hand and went with her to a place only I knew of, over the heath and down the other side where the brambles grew thickly beside a brook. The fruit was fatter and juicier there than anywhere else in the district, for even after the long hot summer the roots could still reach water in the brook. And the spot was far from the village, so that others had not already picked the best of the harvest for their jams and jellies.

A dead branch from a tree had fallen across one of the bushes, conveniently flattening the briars so that we could walk along it and reach the big fruit in the middle of the bush. There was the strong scent of meadowsweet all around us from the damp places beside the water.

Jenny soon tired of picking and ate instead, cramming blackberries into her mouth in great handfuls. And when she tired of eating, she paddled in the brook till her feet were blotchy with cold. A green woodpecker flashed past her into the trees.

'We'll go home now,' I said when the basin was full.

We were about to cross the open heath. I caught sight of a brown creature ahead of us, squatting only half hidden. The tufted grass and speedwell was barely high enough to cover a hare.

'Jenny,' I whispered, pressing her shoulder. 'Keep still.' I myself froze, and Jenny sank to the ground.

It was a doe. A buck would never be foolish enough to linger on open ground, unless it were spring and he was up to his mad antics looking for a mate. She crouched about two hundred yards ahead waiting for her young. There was no wind, so our scent did not carry. But she had a keen sense of sound.

'Lie down, Jenny, lie down. Don't move,' I said.

I would have been glad of my dog with me.

I set the basin down beside Jenny and then began to walk forwards with calm steady strides. I kept walking purposefully across the common towards the doe. She had seen me. She remained motionless, her eye fixed on me. I did not return her gaze, but kept my eye slightly ahead, almost as though I had not seen her.

A hare is a rapid mover. It can travel faster than a dog. But sometimes, if you let it believe you have not seen it, that you intend to walk on, it will remain where it is, hoping to rely on speed alone for a quick escape when necessary.

So I walked on towards her. I was within three yards. I did not look in her eye, nor slow up. I was level with her. I was at arm's length. She did not move. From the side of my eye, I could see her big eye follow me. I pretended to walk past, then, when I was a mere half pace ahead, I lunged at her with both hands, sideways, grabbed her by the scruff of the neck.

She struggled, and kicked with her strong hind legs. But I held her firm. Jenny, seeing that I had her, ran over from the edge of the common.

I broke the doe's neck and hind legs across my knee, and since we were on open ground I quickly tucked the body inside my clothing, so that its hind paws were secured by my belt, and the rest of it hung down inside my trouser leg. I had never seen anybody else up here but it was better to be safe.

Jenny carried the basin of blackberries. I supported the weight of the doe with my hand, and we made our way down the shady path towards home.

But then there was a thundering behind us, like distant guns firing in succession. A gentleman on horseback was approaching at a canter. Not a farmer, but a real gentleman with shiny leather boots up to the thigh. I had never seen his lordship but I knew in an instant that this was him.

The path was steeply banked on either side, too narrow for him to pass unless we clambered up the side out of the way. He reined his horse in close behind us, so close that I feared its great hooves would trample on Jenny.

He shouted down. 'And what the devil are you doing here?'

Instinctively, I put my hand to my trouser pocket. I could feel the doe's body still warm, pressed against my leg. I could feel sticky blood from its nose seeping onto my trousers. I withdrew my hand, the fingers bloody, and fumbled with the blackberries in the basin that Jenny held. I remembered Pa's advice. 'Never go on a job in company. Always work alone.' If I had followed that rule, if I had not Jenny here with me, I could have been up the bank, through the trees and away before his lordship had even caught sight of me.

'What have you *there*? Answer me, boy. There in your hand?'

'Wild fruit, sir.' I held up a handful of berries, the black juice concealing the blood on my hand. 'My sister and I were looking for blackberries, sir.'

Jenny's face crumpled up with fright. She began to cry, letting her mouth hang wide open, showing her tongue and teeth stained purple with the juice. She dropped the basin and all the fruit tumbled into the ferns.

His lordship ignored her crying. But the yells frightened the horse and for a moment its nervous movements distracted his lordship. Or perhaps he didn't know the difference between the colour of juice and the colour of congealing blood. I bent down to gather up the blackberries.

'You know that Wilkins doesn't care for trespassers unsettling the game. Moreover, the season has begun and you are in danger of being shot. I can take no responsibility for trespassers who are accidentally shot.'

'Yes, sir.'

'What's your name, boy?'

Everywhere you went the gentry always wanted to know your name, as though keeping some mental record. Yet we had to know and remember who they were without asking.

'Betts, sir.'

'The poacher's son?'

'He was mistakenly dismissed, sir.'

'Gamekeepers, Betts, can be divided into three classes: good, bad and indifferent. Your father comes into the last category.'

'But it was a gang of ruffians who did it. He wasn't a poacher.' But even as I said it, I realized that I was a liar, just as the rector had told me I was. The evil blood must be rising in me, just as it had in my Pa, and in his uncle before him.

'Tell him to keep off my land. Tell him – and his fellows – that they've been in the habit, under some supposed right of common, of doing my farmers and my keepers great mischief, breaking my fences and gates, stealing my game. I hold the sporting rights of my estate. I'll continue to do so without harassment.'

69

'I can't tell him. He was buried three weeks back.'

'You're well rid of him then. I have never known a man take to poaching through hunger, or spend his ill-gotten gains on his family. The poacher's objects are beer, gambling, riot, and debauchery.'

He turned his horse in the narrow path. Its heavy shoes missed Jenny's bare feet. His lordship took a handful of coins from his pocket, and flung them down to the ground for me. They fell in among the ferns.

'Take those back for your father's widow,' he shouted. 'And keep off my land.'

Then he cantered away down the path.

I stopped searching for shiny black berries and now searched among the ferns for silver money. I found a dozen silver tanners nestling in the damp. I wiped them dry, wrapped them in a big sorrel leaf and put them in my pocket, feeling no gratitude to his lordship, only rage that he should tell *me* where I was not to be, when it was he who had disturbed *my* privacy. The path that led to the bramble bushes was mine. It was *I* who knew every nook and cranny. By right of law and inheritance, it might be thought to be his land. By right of use I knew that it was mine.

Jenny bawled all the way home. I told her to be quiet. 'And will you listen to me now! Everything you've seen this afternoon, everything, is a secret between us. You don't speak a word of it to anyone, not even to Jonas.' Jenny often spent time beside Jonas' box-bed, whispering into his ear. Though Jonas had never spoken a word back, I could take no risk that such a miracle might happen. 'A secret, do you understand?'

Jenny nodded.

Before the blackberry pie, we were to have plain dumpling stew, with just a stick of celery and carrot to flavour it.

'I'll help you mix the dumplings, Alice,' I said. I skinned the hare, out of sight of the house, boned it, buried the fur, and chopped the flesh very small before adding it to the pot, so that we should all benefit from the meat, but Ma could not suspect.

That evening as we ate and I saw lolling Jonas wag his head for more, I felt that I had made up for spilling the flour.

I did not give Ma the silver, but when I went out to collect water for washing the dishes, I hid it under the eaves beside Pa's gun. I had a good use for that money.

As I turned back to the house, there was a rustling in the hedge down by Pit Bottom Lane. I thought it was a stoat, or even the badger I'd seen blundering up the lane two nights before in search of worms. But then there was a low hissing.

'Psst. Psst.'

It was Jo Plumb in his five layers of old coats, bobbing up and down behind the hedge, trying to catch my attention. I could smell him even from ten yards away.

'Pst! Betts' son!' he hissed. I pretended not to hear. But I knew he had seen me reach up under the eaves and suspected something of interest was there. I would have to find a new place for my money and Pa's gun, though no hiding place, however, secret, was safe for long from the eyes of a professional.

'Psst. Anything you catch, I'll take off your hands. Anything you don't need for the home pot, I know the dealer.'

'Go away,' I said through the hedge. He sniffed, cleared his throat and spat back through the fence. He had some horrible habits.

'I'm not interested. Just go,' I said. I didn't want to be muddled up with him, or with middlemen, or dealers. They'd be sure to cheat me, or give me away to the law as a decoy to put the policeman off their own scent.

'What you got there?' Jo Plumb persisted. He could smell silver coins in the same way he could smell a mole.

'Nothing,' I said, and waited till I had heard him go away down the lane, before I went indoors again.

Chapter 8

*A*T first, it seemed best to stick to snaring. It was the simplest and easiest of methods. I could slip from the cottage at nightfall, set two or three snares, go back to bed with Humphrey, get up before dawn to check the snares and nobody was any the wiser. And if Alice suspected that I was adding fresh meat to our vegetables, she said nothing. She did not want to be told anything, for then she would be compelled to stop me.

I was working, not just against Wilkins and the other keepers, but also against other predators. One morning, a stoat had reached the snare before me and sunk his sharp fangs into the dead rabbit's neck and drawn off the warm blood of my kill, leaving the remains of the flesh as white as chicken. Ma would have loved to eat chicken, for chicken was a dainty meat.

I went on up to the big warren where, so Pa had once told, there had been colonies of rabbits living for nearly two hundred years. It was a silvery wet morning, and a thin drizzle began to fall.

I waited, and waited, sure that hunger would drive one out. But it was too damp. Rabbits have more sense than to come out in the wet, unless forced.

I blocked up as many bolt holes of the warren as I could find, with balls of prickly gorse. Then I lit a paraffin rag. When it was smoking well, I stuffed the piece down the main hole. But they must have escaped by another route I did not know about. I did not see a single one.

I was shaking with anger at my own failure as I strode home, empty-handed. As I ran through the wood, a fine cock pheasant strutted boldly in front of me, picking for acorns in the fallen leaves. With a shotgun, I could have taken him easily. I resolved to use Pa's gun as soon as I had cartridges. It had lain unused long enough.

Whatever the facts of the law said to the contrary, I knew now that I was too old for school. I parted from Alice and Humphrey at the bottom of the lane.

'No, please Arthur! Please don't truant today! It's Mr Pooley's tests.'

Mr Pooley had devised his own test, as a Preliminary to the Inspector's Standards, to ensure that we all passed.

'I can't do tests, Alice. You know very well.'

'You only need pass two sums out of four,' Alice said. 'Only *two* and you're through.'

'There'll be the writing and the reading too.'

'But the Standards, Arthur. He's had notice the Inspector's coming any day now. If you don't pass he won't get his six shillings.'

A guinea was in my pocket. I could have paid Mr Pooley his six shillings myself.

'I'll help you, Arthur. I'll sit by you. Mr Pooley *must* get the money for every one of us. He has so little to fund the school. They're taking everything from him.' But she knew as well as I, that no amount of pleading on behalf of poor Mr Pooley's six shillings a head would make any difference to me. Once I had decided to do something, I did it. It was not that I minded failing the test. Nor was I afraid of the Standards, nor even of His Majesty's Inspector. But today, I had something far more important planned than ordinary truanting. I was going to buy cartridges. I knew well enough how to fill my own. But, since Pa's accident, I was going to take no risks of that sort.

While Alice and Humphrey were summoned down the lane by the bell, I ran the mile up to the crossroads in time to ride with the carrier into Reepham Market. He went every week. It was a journey of a couple of hours, allowing for the stops and starts to pick up or set down.

The carrier set me down right in the middle of the market square.

'Be going back at two, or thereabouts,' he said, before urging up the old horse, and disappearing between the swirling traffic of carriages and motorcars.

Never before had I seen such a market, with row upon row of stalls, and huge crowds of shoving people, all eager to spend their money on bales of cloth, and watering-cans, live rabbits, and fancy goods. But it was the poulterers' stalls that chiefly attracted my attention, stocked with such a variety and a quantity of game, woodcock, plover, ready-plucked grouse, pigeons, baskets of plover's eggs, and blue-fleshed turkeys dangling from the striped awnings. I was soon confused by the noise and bustle and, having found my way out of the crowded market and into the narrow streets behind, had to ask my way a great many times. The first person I asked didn't understand what I said, and merely shrugged and hurried on his way. The next gave me an answer that I could barely understand.

Finally, a passer-by said, 'Why, you're standing right in Granary Lane now, lad. Can't you see?' He pointed up to the street sign painted in bold black letters on the side of the house, at first storey level.

I nodded. 'Yes, sir. I didn't see it. Thank you, sir.'

There were so many streets in the city, all looking alike, that they had to have their names written up. After the man had gone, I panicked, for if the gunsmiths too could only be identified by the writing on it, then I should never find it.

The gunsmiths, as it turned out, was easily distinguished even by those such as I who could not read the printed sign above the door, for displayed behind the big plate-glass window were all the necessities for a gentleman's field sports. There were bird decoys, field glasses, a brass game counter, a sporting-gun, dismantled and cased with accessories, a silver powder horn in a velvet-lined box. There were leather gaiters, and a polished leather gun case which I would have liked. It would have kept Pa's shotgun waterproof in its new hiding-place in the nettlebed.

But right in the centre of the window was what I had really come for. The cartridges, of many different colours and sizes, were set out in a marvellous geometric pattern, as beautiful in its own way, as Alice's embroidered writing. There were reds and yellows and browns of the cartridge cases, and circles of silver bullets, and swirling lines of cartridge wads.

I was a long time hovering outside. Two gentlemen entered the shop. Through the window, I saw them make their purchases. Then they came out and went on their way. The shop was empty. I could enter. But at that moment, I saw Mr Wilkins approach down the middle of Granary Lane directly towards me. I darted round a corner and into an alleyway. When at last he stepped out of the gunsmiths, I saw that, though he had the same big red weatherbeaten nose, the same brown tweed suit, and the same bowler hat, he was not Mr Wilkins, but another man in country clothes, who looked similar. But it gave me a good shake up to consider that, though I felt this city to be so far from home, to some folk it might not be.

When the shop was again empty of customers, I braced myself to go in, sidled over to the man behind the counter and asked for my four dozen cartridges.

'For my father. A plague of pigeons been attacking the purple sprouting.' Lying had become an easy habit.

The gunsmith looked at me.

'Hold on a moment,' he said.

He went to the back of the shop. I thought he wouldn't sell them to me, that he had none of that size in stock, that he might call a constable. I wondered if I should leave immediately. But just then, a carriage drew up outside. A gentleman and a young boy stepped down.

The gunsmith hurried out from behind the plush curtain to attend to his new customers.

'Holding a big shoot on the twenty-third,' said the gentleman.

'That'll be over at Eardley, sir?' said the gunsmith.

'Expecting a fine bag.'

'Very good, sir.'

'Be Douglas's first big shoot.'

'Well done, sir!' said the gunsmith to the boy, who blinked nervously.

The assistant was called to deal with me, while, at the request of the gentleman, the cased sporting gun was lifted out from the window display. Then replaced. And another was shown to the lad. He held it clumsily, as though it were too heavy, as though he were afraid it might go off in his hand. He was fitted for several guns, the gunsmith tucking the different sized breech pieces under his arm. Much as I longed to see which he was finally given, I decided it was best not to stay longer than I needed.

By eleven o'clock, my business was finished. With some difficulty, I made my way back to the market square. I had nothing to do now but wait for the carrier at two o'clock. I sat on the kerb and ate my dokey, and the time passed slowly. I had already had more than enough of the city. I wanted to be home.

Across the road, three boys, little older than me, though better dressed for they seemed to be office clerks, tumbled out of the public house and fell about laughing on the pavement. No boys back home would have dared behave like that, unashamedly drunk. The demon drink was one of the rector's favourite talks. Besides, we had no public house in our village, and none of my contemporaries had money to spare for beer, any more than their fathers had.

One of the boys, a little less drunk than the others, noticed me, sitting across the road. He stared. I felt stupid and ignorant. My boots were heavy and clumsy compared to his neat black shoes. His dark striped trousers were narrow and neat. My clothes were roughly made and heavily worn.

He staggered, singing, to where the vegetable refuse from the market was being heaped by a road-sweeper into the gutter. He picked out a rotten apple and threw it at me, half-heartedly.

'Country boy!' he called.

One of his companions picked out an old cabbage leaf and threw it.

'Oaf! Horsey horsey horsey oaf!'

They jeered, but threw with such imprecision that they never scored a hit. I did not dare answer. My country style of speaking, I knew, would only make them laugh more. Besides, this was their territory, not mine. They had a right to claim it, to ward off the intrusion of a stranger. I closed my eyes, and tried not to listen.

Then, a fat stallholder, one of the last to close up, shouted at them to leave me alone.

'You in from the country?' she asked kindly. 'Waiting for your Daddy? Here you are, dear.' She gave me a leftover orange from her stall. I should have received it gladly, gratefully, for it was a good fresh orange, not split or soft or rotten. But she looked at me with pity.

The hatred of Wilkins or the rector I could bear. But such a look of pity felt intolerable. I took the orange from her without even thanking her.

The boys, still bragging and shouting, had lost interest and wandered away.

By half-past two, the carrier had still not appeared. I was frightened to wander far in case I should lose myself completely in the maze of streets, and then miss him altogether. By half-past three dusk was beginning to fall. But the city was not plunged into natural darkness as at home. Instead, it glowed prettily all around. The shops and streets were bright with lamps. I thought how Ma and Alice would have admired it. But for myself I vowed that I would never come back here again if I could help it. The warm night lights in no way compensated for the loudness and hardness of it all. All day, I had seen nothing growing, not a patch of green or a blade of grass. Nothing fresh and alive, unless you counted the cut flowers for sale in the flowersellers' basket. But they were all the bright, gaudy colours of blooms raised unnaturally in a glasshouse.

When at last I heard the carrier's cart rumbling over the cobbles towards me, I almost cried with relief.

'You're back!' said Alice, when I stepped indoors. 'Thank heavens for that. I've been worried sick about you. Wherever have you been?'

'To town,' I said, expecting to astonish her. But she barely showed a flicker of interest. 'Well thank heavens you're back now. Her pains have started. She keeps calling for you. Please go up to her quickly.'

Chapter 9

*I*T shouldn't *be* so long,' said Ma. It was already after midnight and she had been in labour too long. She lay on the bed exhausted, and her face was puffed and damp with sweat. 'You go off to sleep now, Alice. You need the rest. Let Arthur stay.'

'You call me when it's time for Mrs Craske, Arthur,' said Alice. She left us the candle and I sat on the stool by Ma's side.

'This is no thing for a boy to have to do,' she said, taking my hand and giving it a squeeze. 'But with you it's always been all right. You've always been special, you know that don't you, Arthur?'

After that, she didn't talk much. The candle flickered and burned low. Her labour eased off and she dozed. I went to sleep too, sitting on the stool. I hadn't known that I could sleep upright like a bird on a twig. I woke up with terrible backache. The candle had burned out and the room was quite dark. I slid off the stool and lay down on the floor but I didn't sleep again.

Towards dawn, the movements started again. The birds had just begun their first scuffling in the roof.

I was astonished at the hidden effort my small mother had within her. I had once watched a tabby cat give birth in the shed at Keeper's Lodge. Although it had been a great effort for that cat, it hadn't seemed to expend every last ounce of strength as my Ma now did. Without moving from the bed, she was working harder than any man digging a plot or labourer mending the holes in the road. Not just her belly, but every muscle in her entire body was involved in the great struggle to expel the baby. Her shoulders, her back, her neck and head and face all heaved together. She was a living force, the centre of moving life, and as the morning came the whole house was alert to the activity taking place within her. She clenched her teeth, gripped the side of the bed with her hands and quite silently, gasped. Her contorted face looked as though she were in pain, yet she made no sound. I had never seen her like this before, so totally absorbed that she was unaware of the other children, of the time of day, of the domestic chores to be done. I was impressed by such great power.

Alice woke and brought our Ma a drink of milk. We could not give her tea as there was no fire. These days we lit the fire later and later each day as the wood-pile grew lower and lower.

I supported Ma while Alice gave her a drink.

'Does it harm her?' I whispered.

'No, of course not,' Alice said sharply. 'She's done it before for each of us.'

I knew that Alice was afraid, and uncertain about the possibility of Ma's pain. I could stand by and silently admire, but I was not a girl. If I were Alice I would have been afraid of the day when I too would have to live through such an ordeal.

'Will she die?' I whispered, for no person could endure so much and survive. I had seen a poisoned sheep dying in a meadow. Its woolly body had been wracked by seizure after seizure as though they would never end. Finally, the sheep died, not from poisoning, but from exhaustion. But even so, I remembered how the Master of Hounds wouldn't buy the carcass to feed the foxhounds in case they too died.

Alice took the little ones downstairs, and told Humphrey to mind them while she went to fetch Mrs Craske.

Suddenly, Ma cried out. Now there was pain.

'Help me, George!' she said. 'Take it away.'

'I'm not George. I'm Arthur,' I said.

When I had watched that tabby in the straw, another female cat had stayed with her. Throughout the birth, the companion cat had licked the mother cat's stomach in a soothing circular motion. The mother cat seemed to welcome the massage.

As my Ma cried out, I put my hand under the blanket and began to stroke her big belly, gently and firmly like the companion cat. It seemed to help her for when I stopped, she opened her eyes and said, 'Go on, George.'

'I'm Arthur.'

I stayed, stroking and massaging until my hands felt weak and soft like suet pudding. All feeling had gone. I thought they would drop off.

Then Ma was taken by a pain that was so deep even my massaging hands would not ease it. She yelled deep in her throat like an animal.

'Alice, fetch Alice. I think we're nearly there!' she said.

Alice ran up the stairs and took a look under the blanket and pushed me out of the door. 'You'd better go now, Arthur. I wish Mrs Craske would come.'

'But she is. You went for her, didn't you?'

Alice nodded. 'But she weren't there. She's out.'

'Did you write her a message?'

'Yes, I said to come quick.'

We were whispering on the stairs so Ma wouldn't hear. Alice always knew how to do everything, or everything that was women's work. I always trusted her to know. But now she looked so afraid.

'I wish Pa were here,' she said. It was the first and only time since he died that she had said this.

I did not see how Pa could have helped. I remembered on the days when Humphrey and Jonas and finally Jenny were born, our Pa coming in drunk, and bringing a net of limes and a slab of lardy cake for us, and asking all the neighbours in for a drop of beer. But I could not recall him doing anything to assist Ma's labour.

Very hesitantly, Alice went back in to be with Ma.

Knowing how cats litter in the straw wasn't much use to anyone. I wished I could do something more useful, so I ran down Pit Bottom Lane.

Alice's note was still pinned to the door of Mrs Craske's hovel, sodden and limp in the damp air. Somewhere in the village, someone else was struggling with a slow birth or a long death. I went home and sat in the garden with the little ones. Even from outside, the life of the little house seemed to be centred behind the tiny dormer window. It was nearly midday, but the sky was so low that it seemed almost dark enough for evening. There was wood to be chopped and water to be drawn, but I could not bring myself to do anything except wait.

I went indoors to fetch a blanket to put over Jonas who was shivering with cold. I heard a faint high-pitched mewing. Alice shrieked down the stairs, 'Arthur! Come quickly!'

My heart stopped and my stomach turned over. I was certain that our mother was dead. I ran up.

'Light the fire!' Alice ordered. 'At once. Put the kettle to boil.'

'But we're saving fuel.' We never lit the fire till gone five.

'But don't you *see*, you idiot! We've been saving fuel for *this*! For *now*!' Alice's face was bright with a mixture of excitement and exasperation. 'For the *baby*!' And she held it out to me in her arms. It was dark, like black pudding, and streaky and damp with mucus. 'We must keep her warm. It's so cold for her upstairs.'

Our Ma called from the room. I peered round the door. She looked different, still humped in the bed, and her face pale and sagging but with a kind of exhausted peace about her.

'It'll be George.' She turned her head and spoke.

'No, Ma. He's dead, Ma. You know that.'

Ma nodded. 'I mean the little one. We'll call him George, shall we?'

'It's a girl baby, Ma,' said Alice. She took a piece of flannel off the chest by the window and wrapped it round the baby so that only the head showed out.

'Oh, so we can't call her George then, can we?' She seemed disappointed and tears oozed out of her eyes. She no longer wanted me with her in the room. She wanted Alice.

Alice handed the baby to me. 'Just keep it warm till Mrs Craske gets here.'

I carried my new sister carefully downstairs, frightened that I might slip, but not daring to put out a hand for the rail as I needed both to hold her firm.

I sat down in the big kitchen chair that used to be Pa's. It was so curious to have Pa dead one month, and this new child of his born before the year was ended. It was very cold in the kitchen. I hugged the baby against my chest to warm her. I had never before held a living creature that was so new, so untouched and fresh. When Humphrey, Jonas, and Jenny had been born, Pa had locked us out of the house for twelve hours. And when my dog had her first litter, I had not dared go into the shed in case I distressed her. But now, I held the delicate bundle in my arms and it was almost as though I had given birth to her myself. I owned her.

I looked into her crumpled little face, which stared up at me solemnly like an owl, and I felt a great bond of closeness for her, a feeling of tenderness greater than I had felt for any living creature before, even my dog or poor Jonas. She was so tiny, and so perfectly made and so utterly helpless.

I will love you George, I thought. I will care for you. I will protect you. I am the man of this house. I shall be the provider of your warmth and food.

'Humphrey!' I ordered. 'See to the fire!' He wanted to hold the baby but I wouldn't allow him to. 'She's too young,' I said, holding her closer. 'You might drop her. She's not even an hour old yet.' Even as I watched, her crumpled face seemed to take recognizable shape and meaning. 'You hurry up with that fire. She's getting cold.'

He obeyed reluctantly and ran for wood and matches.

I tried to remember how it used to be at Keeper's Lodge where we had had a fire ablaze all day, winter and summer. The grate was never left to grow cold from one lighting to the next. We had scarcely any need of kindling.

First thing in the morning, Pa would put just one or two sticks into the warm ash and stir them about. Within minutes a fire was alight from the red heat still there beneath the grey.

'Do you remember, Humphrey, how Pa used to start the fire with just a couple of twigs?' I said.

Humphrey didn't remember.

These days, the fire had to be coaxed, and blown, and begged and pleaded with. And finally, if you were patient, came acrid smoke, and sizzling and a little leap of feeble flame that one urged to grow but did not dare fan for fear of puffing it out altogether.

Today, poor Humphrey had no luck with it. It would not draw up. Instead, he managed to make a cloud of damp smoke which billowed out and made his eyes stream. So I had to let him hold the baby after all, while I saw to it. But I took her back as soon as there was the first sign of red. I told Humphrey to boil water and fill a bowl, and fetch clean cloth. Then I held the baby while he washed her eyes, and her face, and the soft yellow down on her smooth head. By the time we had finished, her skin was no longer purple, but had softened to a smooth creamy white like wax candles.

We did not wash the rest of her body as I was afraid of hurting the fleshy cord, still attached to her stomach. Mrs Craske would see to that. We just wrapped her in another knitted blanket, and I continued to nurse her by the fire, while Humphrey stirred a pan of gruel for Ma.

I sang to her and when she turned her head from side to side like a kitten rootling for milk in its mother's furry belly,

I let Humphrey put his little finger in her mouth to suck.

It grew dark and we remembered to bring Jonas, damp with dew, in from the garden and set him in his box.

Jenny came in and did not at first see what we had. She tugged at the blanket and tried to climb onto my lap. Then she saw the baby and she prodded at it, and touched its nose. But she tired of this and wanted our Ma.

'No, Mumma's sleeping,' said Humphrey. 'Mumma's tired.'

Jenny began to cry and wail and kick the door with her small bare feet. So Humphrey picked her up and took her out for a piggy-back ride down the dark lane.

When Mrs Craske arrived, she snatched the baby from me and made disapproving clicking noises about the untidy way in which I had wrapped the cloth around her. But I didn't mind. I knew that the baby was mine really.

After scolding me, Mrs Craske went and scolded Alice for the way she had severed the cord. But Alice didn't seem to mind either. She was almost drunk with excitement.

'I did it,' she smiled. 'I saw her born. I got her born all by myself.'

Within the week, we received the parish box of infant clothes. They were ours to keep until Georgina was three months old, when they must be returned, properly laundered, mended and ironed, to the rectory. The baby was strong and healthy. She grew rapidly and quickly became too large for the tiny gowns. But Ma was slow to regain her strength. The Benevolent Society provided us with cod liver oil, and a bottle of porter for her, and I used some of my secret supply of his lordship's money to fetch her extra provisions from the village, for Mrs Craske said Ma should have eggs and white bread.

When I came out of the village store clutching the loaf and two eggs, I was confronted with the rector.

Whenever I met that man, a coldness grabbed me by the throat.

'The new child has not yet been baptized,' he said, without acknowledging my 'Good Morning'. 'The unbaptized will go to hell. You will convey my message to your mother.'

Of course Baby Georgina must be saved from the sulphur fires of hell. But what, I wanted to ask, about my Pa? Suppose he had not been baptized. I remembered how keenly Ma had insisted that we all bid him goodbye. Had he gone to hell now?

Ma was not well enough to leave home. But on the following Saturday, Alice wrapped Georgina warmly in as many clothes of Jenny's that would fit, and the rest of us took her down to church.

Alice and I made the responses for godparents, renouncing The Devil and all his works and all covetous desires of the world, and promising solemnly on the baby's behalf to walk obediently in God's holy will all the days of our lives.

Outside the church, the rector's two little children played on the gravestones, waiting for their father to finish disrobing. Jenny toddled over to join them. Alice called her back. Jenny had not yet learned that the children of labourers do not mix with the children of other classes.

Alice glanced at them disapprovingly.

'They should know better than that. Climbing all over the graves of the dead.'

Our Pa's grave had no stone to mark his place. Three more dead had been buried since, and now the brown earthy mounds all looked quite alike.

'Come on, hurry up!' said Alice. 'Baby's fretting for her pap.'

As we hurried past the rector's children, I noticed their strange faces, scarlet and mottled. And they both had swollen watering eyes.

Chapter 10

So Jenny was the first to fall. She coughed all night, a hard dry cough. Next day, she was feverish and we saw the irregular blotchy rash on her face and neck. Her eyes were red and watering like the rector's children. She cried from the pain in her head.

'That's the measles, Mrs Betts,' said Mrs Craske, as she pulled back Jenny's petticoat with her long dirty fingers, to reveal the rash spreading downwards like a red sea over Jenny's whole body.

'I don't doubt any of them can escape it now. Try her with blackcurrant tea,' said Mrs Craske. 'And inhalations if the breathing's bad.'

The breathing was very bad and in the night, I heard from the rapid panting and the restlessness as he tossed and gabbled nonsense in bed beside me, that Humphrey had fallen too. Then Alice, and me, and Jonas, till we were all sick with the measles. Ma too had high fever and the florid rash. There was nobody to draw water, or set the fire.

We all lay upstairs, united in a shared infection, yet each alone inside the private terrors of delirium. I was chased, again and again, by Wilkins. Whenever he came close, he turned into my Pa. As I ran forward to embrace him, there would be the sound of a shot, and the side of his head fell away.

Through the mist of fever, I saw Mrs Craske come to the loft and cool our heads with a wet cloth. She held out for me a can of cold water from which to sip. I felt her place a poultice of thick paper and lard on my chest and bind it tightly with a strip of bandage. Filthy though I knew her hands to be, rank though the water was, for she did not strain it through muslin like our Ma, I was silently grateful for her care.

Dimly, I saw her darken the gloomy room still more by hanging a heavy sack across the window, and I felt such relief that one symptom at least – the sharp pain behind my eyes – was relieved. I smelled the coal-tar lamp she burned to ease Jenny's harsh cough. And for all of us, our common fever was marked by the constant time-keeping of Jonas whimpering.

Only the baby did not fall ill. I heard Mrs Craske taking her away, then Mrs Craske bring her back and place her in bed beside our Ma for her feed. Then she took her away. I knew that Ma must be very ill to allow Georgina to remain for even an hour in Mrs Craske's filthy hovel, let alone spend the nights there.

Mine was the mildest case, at any rate I was the first to recover. I awoke not wet with sweat, but feeling almost fresh as from a normal sleep. The pain had gone from behind my eyes, and the aching from my limbs. I heard wind rustling through holes in the roof. It was afternoon, and when I lifted the flap of sack over the window, there was a bleak sullen landscape, devoid of all movement or colour. But after the hideous nightmare countryside of my dreams, it seemed safe and reassuring. I stumbled downstairs to see to the fire. The chopper was lost. I had left it out before we all were ill, meaning to bring it in. I had forgotten. I searched in the fading light, kicking up damp sawdust and clods of heavy soil, but finding nothing. In the end I had to resort to breaking small branches with my bare hands. I did not find the chopper but in my search I did find half a dozen potato tubers which we had overlooked in the autumn. As I carried them in to cook Mrs Craske came up the path with the baby.

'Ah! I see you're well again,' she said.

I wanted to protest that I was not fully better. By now my legs felt like wet straw and my head was beginning to throb again from the effort. But there was no wasted sympathy from Mrs Craske.

'Take baby to your mother for her feed. After, give baby some breadsop, and make tea, with plenty of sugar, for your mother. She must keep up her strength. And when you've seen to the fire, put some warm hearth ashes in a pot by your mother's feet.'

'We have no sugar,' I said. But otherwise, I did as I was told.

The others recovered gradually and one by one came downstairs to huddle by the grate where I tried to keep the fire going. Only Jonas did not recover. All the good health and strength, which had been built up in him through the summer, seemed suddenly drained out of him like blood drained from meat, leaving him grey and pinched.

Mrs Craske came again and gave us a dose of nettle tea to cool our blood after the fever.

'Mine's cold enough already,' said Humphrey, 'without needing cooling.'

Mrs Craske gave Jonas a tonic of quinine and rose-leaves followed by a spoonful of the baby's laudanum to lull him to sleep so that Ma could get some rest. But he moaned on as before and then began to have fits. Ma said it was the fever had set something off in his brain. He jerked in his box-bed, and his head went back. His eyes rolled and his thin legs twitched while he uttered strange cries. Jenny sat beside him and watched.

Afterwards, he always slept for several hours. The fits induced in him a deeper sleep than all Mrs Craske's spoonfuls of Godfrey's cordial.

She came again and prodded him, and felt his stomach and forced open his mouth and looked at his tongue. Then she shook her head.

'What did I tell you?' she muttered. 'The bird.'

'What bird?' I said.

'A sparrow came into the kitchen yesterday,' said Humphrey. 'And flew round three times.'

'We don't hold with any of that nonsense,' said Alice.

'She said there'll be a death,' said Humphrey.

'Nonsense, there's always been birds in and out of this house. They live in the thatch.'

Mrs Craske refused to accept the usual payment.

Ma called the doctor. His visit cost ten shillings. We all knew that he came too late. Bird or no bird, Jonas was visibly fading. But to maintain her reputation Ma wanted him to be seen to call, even if it cost her the last shillings she had.

It cost more than that, for we had no shillings left.

The doctor said grudgingly, 'Never mind, Mrs Betts. I can claim from the Benevolent Fund.'

Ma did not want charity from the parish, but since she had not the money to pay him, there was nothing she could do to stop him.

Jonas died on Ash Wednesday. Ma and Alice cried as they cleaned and wrapped his body. But I did not really mourn him. It was a relief not to have to see his unsmiling, pinched little face and to have to hear his sad whimpering every time you stepped indoors.

Jonas' burial cost another two pounds ten shillings which we did not have, though the rector let Ma have the tolling of the bell for nothing. She was anxious to have the tolling. I think she thought it made the mourning more real.

Either bereavement, or the continuing cold, affected everybody's thinking, so that we were all sluggish and slow. It was an effort to move. Ma crouched by the grate with the baby at her breast. Jenny developed chilblains on her feet which she picked at and rubbed all day so they were red and weeping. Humphrey had chilblains on his face.

We were without tea or sugar all month. But there were three good events. Baby learned to sit up and was moved into Jonas' box-bed, I found the wood-chopper hanging in its proper place on a nail in the shed, and I shot a grey lag goose.

I had slipped out early one morning with Pa's gun, intending to take a pheasant or a rabbit. The ground was wet and there was a thin white mist over everything, so that the world seemed closed and quiet. All sounds were distorted.

Suddenly, I heard a cry like wailing dogs in the sky. Blundering through the vapour towards me with a laborious beating of wings, came the goose, flying alone, its long neck outstretched. I raised the gun to my shoulder, pulled back the hammer, and took aim. My heart was beating in my chest. The bird was so large, and it had flown such a long way that it seemed to bring the breath of frozen North with it. When it was close enough for me to see quite clearly its pink feet tucked under, and the bright orange bill, I fired, just a fraction ahead of its flight-path. It was a big bird, eight or ten pounds, and tumbled heavily to earth, and lay crumpled in the grass with a trickle of blood oozing from its bill.

In the kitchen Alice took the bird without a word, either of approval or displeasure, sat down with it grasped firmly between her knees, and plucked out the grey feathers. She put her hand into the body cavity and drew out the innards. It was an old bird. Its flesh was dark and its feet stiff. She cut off the feet and head, and left a loose flap of skin at the neck, to turn under to prevent the stuffing falling out. But we had no real stuffing, so she put an onion and an apple inside. Plucking a bird leaves a great mess of down and feathers. If you burn them, they smell bad. So I took them all, and dug a hole and buried them.

Alice roasted the goose in the oven, and though there was no pork fat left to baste it, the meat was rich enough in its own yellow fat, to cook nice and moist. We had none of us eaten goose before. It had a strange stringy taste which was not altogether pleasant. We ate our meal in silence, as though a common guilt, knowing what we ate, affected the whole family.

But we needed more than meat to keep us alive. We needed candles and milk. Jenny had no shoes, nor ever had had. We needed oil for the lamp, ground rice and arrowroot for the baby, for it was well past the time for her to be weaned. For all these things, we needed money in the jar, not rich dark meat.

I resolved, reluctantly, to find and use the experience of Joseph Plumb. He was forever totting and foraging somewhere.

I found him in a turnip-field, supposedly about his business of mole-catching. He didn't use the mole-trap but sat quiet on the edge of a field where his ragged garments blended easily into the crisscross of the hawthorn hedge. He kept his eyes fixed on the field until he saw a mole-hill rising, then he leaped across the ground to where the earth was being thrown up and made his catch.

He seemed unsurprised when I sat down beside him to wait and asked no explanation.

'I knew you'd come to me in time,' he said, and laughed. 'Moles move at the chiming hours. Four, eight, and twelve of the clock. They'll go hunting worms at dawn. Night dew brings worms up to the surface.'

He scrumped a handful of green turnip tops which he stuffed inside his hat-band, before gathering up the dead moles into a sack to take to the farmer. He was paid threepence a head for them.

'Sure cure for weak bladder, mole. Eat him cooked, never have the trouble again.'

I had never had a weak bladder so did not need to follow his advice. His other advice I took eagerly.

He was a natural poacher and worked by instinct. If there was a feathered bird in a tree, or a creature in the grass, he knew of its whereabouts. Over the days, he showed me his skill with a gate net, a long net, a whistle, and a kite. He knew how to draw a rabbit from a hole by hypnosis.

He had gathered all the ways there were of taking game, and of disposing of it too, not just by selling it, but as bribes to the policeman, or the magistrates to keep himself out of gaol. Sometimes he sold directly, and for a better price, to the cook of a large doctor's house in town.

Unlike my Pa who had raged at the corruption of the world, Jo Plumb saw no differences in the two sides of the law.

'There's many a man on the bench takes a fancy to a bit of golden-feather now and then,' he said. 'And can you blame him? You know too, I've always had the idea that game is as much mine as anybody else's.

It frightened me, sometimes, listening to him. He said some things that I didn't understand, like having to feel you were a bird yourself, or like knowing the birds like God knowed them.

I tried to ask Alice about it. She read so much, especially the Bible, I felt sure she must be able to explain, though of course I didn't say it was Joseph Plumb I'd been talking to. But she was shocked all the same.

'That's sacrilege!' she said. 'What makes you *think* up such things, Arthur? It's wrong and wicked to say *anything* feels like God, except God Himself.'

Joseph Plumb was arrogant. Often he boasted to me about the things he'd done, all the game he'd taken.

'Red grouse, ptarmigan, black grouse, capercaillie, swans, geese, or ducks. Caught them all in my time. Saw you took a grey lag the other day. Heard the shot right over four acres. You ought to be more stealthy.'

I did not know I had been heard that night. His tiny eyes glinted under the shadow of his hat. 'Could have found you thirty bob or more for that bird, if you'd only brung him me. Next time you'll know. Whatever you find, you'll bring to me. Right, laddo?'

I nodded.

Sometimes we got so many birds, I could scarcely walk for the weight of them round my waist, and was sweating all night from the heavy work. Even what I caught on my own I took to Jo Plumb.

Between us, we took a fair bounty of mixed game. But one night when I met up with him at our usual rendezvous he was rolling drunk, snorting and roaring like a wild thing as he came through the wood. He had spent all our money on beer. There wasn't even a sixpence left for me.

'Come on, laddo,' he grunted. 'We'll be on our way then. Heard there's some of them longtails up Wigden's Way.'

I did not want to be with him. There was no knowing what he might get up to in that unstable condition. Stumbling through the trees, falling against fences, fumbling with his net, he would give us both away.

He wasn't to be dropped so easily. He came by next evening as I helped Humphrey carry in water to the kitchen. I saw the brown tattery rags in our shed like some old bundle hung on a hook. He might have been waiting there all day.

As Humphrey was with me, I pretended not to see him. Later, on the pretext of collecting a bundle of sticks I went out. I guessed by the smell of dead chickens and rotting leaves that he was still there.

'Well, what is it you want?' I asked into the shadows, though I knew well enough. He wanted my youth and strength to spare himself the effort on his rounds. He wanted the use of my Pa's gun.

'I been waiting for you all night, Betts' son, up Makin's Wood way.'

'And I've been waiting for you to pay up what you owe,' I said.

'I'm master of the woods round here. I pay when I pay.' He spat noisily and deeply into the woodpile.

'Go away then,' I said. 'You can keep away from our place till you act honestly.'

'*Our* place!' he laughed. 'Think you own it. Lease runs out in Spring. Who'll pay your rent then? Will it be *your* place come Maytime?'

He came every evening for the next week, but in the end he stopped bothering me.

My Pa had been quite right. I should have never tried to work in a twosome.

Chapter 11

THERE is a gentleness about the colour of early spring before the leaves have started to show. I went down to Neil's Grove, beyond Neil's Farm. In pale sunlight, the bark of the beech trees, the dry bare ground, and the sky showing between the grey twigs shared the same silvery sheen.

As I went through the undergrowth, becoming part of the wood, I felt myself absorb some of that invisible radiance. There were fresh rabbit droppings on a pathway. Underfoot I saw the pale tips of lent lilies pushing through the dry leaves.

I had lately become both more cunning and more confident. I knew where to go, what and who to avoid. I knew precisely what time the underkeepers went their rounds, what time each went in for his breakfast. I knew I still had a great deal more to learn. I must study the weather, and all the signs of woodcraft, and the call of the birds, and I must be able to distinguish the different sounds of the woods. For I had it in mind to become a professional poacher, even though it might mean that soon I would have to leave home and live away from Ma and the little ones so as not to implicate them in any way. Perhaps, in my dreams, I had become over-confident.

I jumped a stream which runs through Neil's Grove. I made no noise, yet suddenly, with a massive flapping of wings like the dull thud of blocks beating, a flight of woodpigeons high overhead, flew out of the wood. I should have been warned by their signal that I wasn't alone. But the exhilaration of the day was in me. I took no warning and went on my round.

With three shots, I took one pheasant for cash, and two rabbits for home. I was oblivious of trackers.

I followed a mossy track, keeping low, intending to hide my catch in a disused burrow till evening, and Pa's gun in a bramble-bed. I changed its hiding place every few days. I slithered under a gate, dragging the game and gun beside me, and was confronted with a pair of brown gaitered legs astride the track.

Mr Wilkins and a constable barred my exit from the wood. Mr Wilkins' pointer bounded forward and sniffed hopefully at my face. Mr Wilkins' gun was fully cocked, the double barrels directly trained on me as though I was some vermin about to be destroyed. I scrambled to my feet and Mr Wilkins seized one of my hands, as though he would bid me good-day. Instead, he held my fingers up to his big nose and sniffed.

'Gunpowder,' he nodded to the policeman.

There was no need for such a show of cleverness since I had the game with me. The policeman took it from me, and the gun.

'I summons you, Betts, for having game in your possession, unlawfully obtained,' he said.

I could not deny it, so I said nothing.

I was led into court handcuffed to the constable, as though I were a real criminal and might run away. As I was small for my age and he was a burly man, it was an uncomfortable lop-sided walk for both. At first, the crowd in the courtroom stared but to my relief, quickly lost interest. Among the strangers, I was surprised to see the familiar, if not entirely welcome, faces of Mr Pooley and the rector.

Mr Pooley had come to speak up in my defence, how I was a good boy who had been badly influenced, how I came from a poor but honest family, how this was my first offence.

Mr Pooley's speech did me little good for, soon after, the rector spoke. He brought up every misdemeanour I had ever done, including truancy. He had brought with him the black book from Mr Pooley's school cupboard and he read out from it. The number of my attendances in school that year, seemed few, even to me.

'Your honour, for his own good the youth's continued truancy, disobedience and dishonesty must all be taken into account. All my life, I have struggled in the parish to let the labouring classes see that they depend on the observance of the decencies of life and fine moral conduct for the means of employment.'

Mr Pooley suddenly stood up, indignant, his hat in hand.

'There are too many wealthy people,' he shouted across the courtroom, 'who have no other means of procuring game, except by purchase.' I do not think it was his turn to speak, for the magistrate looked startled. 'It is at *their* feet we must lay blame. It is *their* habits which necessarily encourage illegal sportsmanship among boys such as Arthur.'

The rector turned, from the magistrate whom he had been addressing, to Mr Pooley. His little birdy eyes were black with anger.

'You forget, Pooley, that the object and purpose of the laws of this land are not entirely confined to restraining our ignorant and rustic population from its clandestine activities. They are also there to protect our wild game. And the qualified sportsman is *equally* restrained from killing game at the incorrect season. Why should these laws be applied only to those who hold accredited sporting rights? Why should the labouring classes not be subject to the same laws? Your honour, I have seen in my time a young gentleman of good breeding whipped raw for taking a pheasant out-of-season. You may mark my words, he never again made *that* mistake!'

They argued away. But I gave up trying to follow what they said. The whole process seemed to have little to do with me.

The magistrate, perplexed at the unexpected unruliness of his court, finally regained control and summed up.

'It is an odd thing, I have seen it before. Congenital poachers will father poachers. When hunting is in the blood, you see a child put his natural cunning to stalking and outwitting game. But in your case,' he turned to me, 'we are fortunate to see that the child has *not* outwitted us!' He smiled. 'You are fortunate, young man, to have such people in your village prepared to stand up for you and consider your welfare. You have not escaped justice. By prudent punishment you may yet be saved.'

The sentence was one month's imprisonment or ten pounds' fine. I felt a glow on my cheeks that I should be worth so much.

'Yes, sir. Thank you, sir. Betts, sir.' I said. They always wanted to know your name. It seemed as well to give it yet again. But after sentence, I was not supposed to say anything.

I was taken below.

In the cell I waited, alone, for the rest of the day. I supposed, I should soon be taken to prison. My wrists were sore and I hoped I should not be handcuffed again to a tall policeman. I was not frightened, for at least I knew that I was not going to suffer the ultimate penalty of transportation, like my great uncle, to the land of black men who grow oranges.

In the evening a warden unlocked the door and told me I could go home. My gun was returned to me.

'Your fine's been paid,' he said gruffly. 'Good job too.'

'Who paid it?'

'Been paid off. Isn't that enough? Now be off.' He handed me half a crown for the fare home.

Since there was no means of transport on which to spend

the half crown, I found my way through the narrow confusing streets of Reepham Market on foot. I wanted to stop and spend the half crown at a pie-stall just beyond the prison gates, or on a glass of stout in a pub. But with a shotgun under my arm, I knew I stood a high chance of re-arrest. I went into an alley, and slid the barrel down the inside of my trouser leg. Although this greatly impeded my walk, I was less conspicious. I did not remove it until I was well beyond the city and out into open fields again. The night air was good to breathe.

I walked all night. It was too cold to lie down and sleep in a hedge. Towards dawn I reached Pit Bottom Lane, uncertain what reception would greet me. I knew I should not be a hero, but some consideration for my brief stay in prison and long walk home I did at least hope for.

What I did not expect was the combined fury of both Ma and Alice. As they heard me enter the cold kitchen, they were down from the loft as angry as a nest of disturbed fledglings.

'So you're back!' said Ma, her hands on her hips. 'Then you'll get straight down there and say thank you.'

I was almost faint with hunger, having eating nothing but a dishful of prison porridge the morning before.

'You cause us all this trouble and worry, and the first thing you can think of is your own stomach,' she shrieked at me. 'You'll go and say thank you before you do anything else, my boy,' and she gave me a slap across the head.

'To whom? For what?'

'To Mrs Craske, you idiot!' hissed Alice, her eyes bright and hard like the angry owl. 'For paying off your fine.'

'Never, ever, have I had to suffer such shame,' said my Ma. 'Never before have I had to be so indebted. And to a woman like that. We'll never pay it back. I know we shan't.'

I went miserably and hungrily down the lane and tapped on Mrs Craske's door. She was a long time answering. She opened her window a crack and peered out. Her hair looked like dirty black string. Her shawl was as filthy as ever. She stared at me as though she had no idea who I was. I thanked her as well as I could. Ten pounds was such a tidy sum that it was hard to find the right words. She listened and smiled her dreadful smile with the bare gums.

'Well don't do it again or you'll have your mother die of worry,' she said and pulled the window shut.

I was free for two weeks. But they were determined to have me by some means or another. It was the School Attendance Officer who was after me next.

The false spring was over. There was a mean penetrating wind blowing from the north east. I took shelter from the driving wind and rain, in a disused barn. It was draughty, but not as cold as working out in the open all day. My supply of copper snares had long since run out, but I decided not to use the gun again for a while, until things had quietened. I had some strands of horse-hair which I was attempting to knot into invisible snares as I had seen Jo Plumb do. They were fine enough to be almost invisible, yet strong enough, so I hoped, to withstand the pull and thrust of a full-sized rabbit, if not a hare.

The noise of wind, the drumming of rain on the brown field blocked out all other sound. So I heard nothing of the Attendance Officer until I glanced up and saw him silhouetted in the entrance to the barn. He was strangely dressed for the countryside in a frock-coat and silk hat. His narrow trousers were ruined with mud.

As soon as I had overcome my astonishment at seeing him, I tried to bolt for it between his legs, then to the side of him. But he had me in an instant by the scruff of the neck. I could not imagine how he had located me in the barn. There was no footpath. You had to cross several open fields and climb through a hedge. Nobody knew I was there, not even Alice. Nobody, that is, except Jo Plumb.

My Pa was so right. A professional poacher is never to be trusted. He'll do anything for money.

As the truant man and I went back across those three muddy fields, facing into the lashing rain, and gathering great clods of wet earth on our boots, I looked round all the time to see if I could catch a glimpse of Jo Plumb's tatty, bird-stained hat, or his torn coat bobbing along beneath a hedgerow, just to reassure myself that it was not by chance alone that I had been taken. But of course, I saw nothing. He would be far away by now.

I struggled and kicked and bit the Officer's hand every so often to show that I was not to be taken as easily as a kitten.

This time, there was no trial. He already had a warrant for me, and a covered cart already waiting at the crossroads. The back was unlocked, and I was flung in with such force that my lip hit the wooden floor and split. I had seen dead game laid in the back of a cart with more gentleness than the Attendance Officer showed me.

He was clearly doing the rounds of the county, for there were two miserable looking lads already huddled in the cart. One was a cringing spotty youth, older and taller than me, who, he revealed with pride, had been caught stealing coal from an old woman. He was no more than a petty thief. I resolved not to speak with him again. The other little chap seemed scarcely older than Jenny. Like me, he was a persistent truanter. We were all three taken to the school of correction for truanters and other misfits.

We were bundled by the Attendance Officer into the cold and gloomy hall of Reform School. I felt ready to cry. We heard the studded door locked behind us with an iron bolt but dared not look round to see.

'Turn out your pockets,' said the warden in charge.

I did so. There was not much in them, the few strands of horse-hair, some round stones for my catapult, a piece of bread, and a shrivelled yellow apple which had been my breakfast.

'Why haven't you eaten this?' the warden asked. His job was to make a list of the contents of our pockets.

I was too frightened to explain that being arrested first thing in the morning takes away your appetite. When I did not reply, he took the apple and put it in a drawer of his desk, and closed it. I noticed several other edible treasures in there, a packet of tea, some raisins, and a bar of chocolate. He marked down the other items from my pocket in a book, which the Attendance Officer witnessed with his signature, but no note was made of my yellow apple.

'Strip off,' the warden said, when he had finished with the book.

I didn't understand. I was too frightened and too tired to move.

'Strip!' he bawled, pulling at my shirt. 'Your clothes! Take 'em off. You deaf or something?'

The other two lads had begun to undress.

Standing in the open hall, with the Attendance Officer and the warden looking on, we had to undress till we were quite naked. Then the warden looked all over our bodies to see if there were any marks or injuries. There were none, on me, apart from the chaffed wrist from the handcuff a fortnight previously, but he did not write that down. He noted the colour of my eyes, and my hair and my age. And he guessed at my weight.

When it was the turn of the tall lad, he protested that his age had been incorrectly written down.

'I'm fourteen, not thirteen,' he said.

'Sir,' said the warden.

'Not thirteen. You've written thirteen,' the boy persisted.

'Sir,' the warden repeated. 'I'm not thirteen, *sir*, is what you say, should you have something of importance to say, which I very much doubt.'

In the book he left the age as thirteen. I could see that whether the lad was thirteen, or fourteen, or thirty or forty, or only three or four, was of no real interest to him whatsoever. His job was to fill up the columns.

The Attendance Officer signed the book and left. We were

shoved, still naked, down a passage and locked, each alone, into a separate room. I trembled with fear and cold not knowing what was to happen next.

A tin bath was dragged in, and filled with cold water. The warden searched my head for vermin. He seemed astonished to find none, and tugged tufts of my hair this way and that, and pulled my ears in his search. Then I was made to wash with hard yellow soap like a brick in the tub of cold water. Finally, I was given a set of harsh grey clothes, stiff like boards, and a pair of socks which had been darned so many times that they were more like thick grey cobwebs.

It was the last bath I had alone, for after that we bathed twenty at a time, supervised by the Labour Master, who hovered in the cold bathhouse with a wet towel ready to swipe out at us whenever he could. There were a hundred and twenty boys in the Reform School, boys who had stolen as little as a bag of turnips, or as much as a hundred pounds. There was even a boy who had murdered. But none of us were heroes.

'You are the ruin of the country. No pride in your nation, or yourselves. You just wish to take, take, take, take.' At each 'take' the Labour Master hit out with the wet knotted towel. 'Taking all you can.'

After the daily cold bath, we were marched to the dormitories and waited for the order to undress. Then, we stood to attention and awaited the order to fold our clothes. We waited, to attention, at the foot of the bed, for the order to get in. The lights were put out, and it was silence.

At six, the new day began with a clanging of bells, and a shouting of orders. We dressed, and washed, again by order, and lined up by our beds for inspection. The slightest sign of wet on any bed and the boy had to remain standing where he was while the others filed downstairs to spend half an hour on knees in chapel.

There is something about sharing a bed with your brother

all your life that encourages one to be dry from an early age. But some of my fellows, young and old, were not so lucky. Little Jamie, who arrived the same day as I, had accidents in his bed night after night. Each bed-wetter had his mattress tied to his back. Then they were all marched down to the yard where they paraded round in a circle until the palliasses were dry. If it rained the punishment was the same, so that by the end of the day the mattress was wetter still. Breakfast was porridge and a tin mug of cocoa made with water. Afterwards, we lined up again to be given our duties of the day by the Labour Master: scrubbing floors and kitchen tables, mopping out the latrines, darning the socks, preparing food. Dinner was half a pint of stirabout made from oatmeal, and maizemeal mixed with water and baked in an oven. Even in our worst poverty at Pit Bottom, I had never before had to eat such stuff. Yet now I devoured it eagerly. It seemed almost the best part of the day.

School truanters under fourteen spent most of the day in the classroom, where we learned nothing. The teacher's chief concern was, not to each us the three R's but to instil discipline, which he did either by shouting at us or by forcing us to sit with our hands on heads. Both he and the Labour Master inflicted indignation and cruelty on the boys for the sheer pleasure of seeing us cry.

At the end of the first week, I heard my name called out at assembly.

'Betts, step forward.'

I knew at once that my turn had come for that day's birching.

Slouching, rudeness, lateness into class, were all punishable by beating. We all knew the code. Six for slouching, twelve for rudeness, twelve for blasphemy, and profane language.

I had done none of these things. I had kept myself inconspicuous. I was trying to live out my time in Reform School as though I were stalking my Pa through Great

Wood on a still evening, silently and invisibly so that no one would see me. My good behaviour did not render me entirely invisible. All boys had to take their turn. And if it were not today, it would be another. If it were not me, it would be another like me.

'Step up, Betts. You heard. Step up.' The Labour Master thwacked the cane impatiently against his thigh as though he had not time to waste.

I had suffered pain before. When I cut my hand on Pa's chopper, when I stumbled and gashed my knee, when bitten by a stoat. But those pains had the element of surprise and chance so that you were caught unawares.

This was pain premeditated and tinged with fear. Waiting for the cane to descend, doubled up, my head hung down, so that all the blood seemed to rush like a stream into my brain, scarcely able to breathe, trembling with anticipation, yet not daring to seem afraid. My Pa's two beatings with the belt seemed just and gentle compared to this.

When it was done my fellows half dragged me, for my legs were like bread and milk and scarcely fit for walking, to the dormitory and laid me face down on the bed. They took off my boots and loosened my belt, but I begged them not to touch my shirt for it gave me such terrible pain to move my arms. My back seemed to be on fire.

I must have slept for the rest of the day for I dreamed repeatedly of a rabbit I had once come across in a badly set trap. The noose had slipped and strangled, not the rabbit's head, but its hindquarters. Its legs and haunches were raw and bloody with struggling to escape. Sometimes, in my dream, I became that rabbit. It was *my* back and legs which were raw and screaming hot. Sometimes, I dreamed it as it was. I had at once taken a stone to its head and killed it outright so that its suffering was instantly over and it lay still. I remembered how I had not taken it home for I could not bear to think of us eating a creature which had died so slowly and ignobly. But now, in the dream, it did not die but continued to writhe with its great round bulging eyes open and rolling with pain.

When I awoke next, it was night. My face was wet with tears. The dormitory was in silence. One of the boys knelt by my bed. It was Jamie. Once, when he had wept after a beating, I had comforted him and told him the story of my dog to take his mind off himself.

He pressed a piece of cold grey potato into my hand, saved from supper. I was not hungry. I did not want potato. I wanted water, for the pain across my back had given me a terrible thirst. But I ate his gift lest it should be found in the morning by the housekeeper, and Jamie's reward for kindness to me would be a beating for stealing from the dining-table.

When I awoke in the morning I found my lips cracked and my eyes swollen from crying in my sleep. I had cried for the smell of sweet fresh air, for the sight of a ploughed field, the chatter of a reed bunting, the spasmodic cackling of the cock pheasants in the copse behind our cottage. As I turned my head I imagined I could hear the low beat of wings flying over my head. But I was merely deceived by the rattle of a window pane, and the creak of the Labour Master's feet as he came on his rounds to order us out of bed. He strode directly to the foot of my bed, I was already out of it and standing to attention by the side as we had to do.

'Betts. What is wrong with your face?'

'Nothing sir.'

'Liar. It's revolting.' He hit me. 'You've been crying.'

'Yes, sir.'

'You've not come here to blub for your mummy. You are here that your ignorance may be transformed to some useful employment.' He hit me again. 'You will be on latrine duty for seven days. You are here to be made a man.'

From that day, I vowed that I would not cry again, neither in the privacy of my bed, nor in the ignorance of sleep.

Chapter 12

GRUDGINGLY, the Labour Master handed me Alice's first letter as we assembled for morning prayers. It was the only letter I had ever received in my life and I scarcely knew what to do with it. I turned the envelope over. It had already been opened and read, either by the warden, or the Governor, or the Labour Master. The envelope was torn and crumpled, and the letter itself roughly folded inside.

'All incoming mail is to be read out loud,' said the Labour Master. 'So that we might all share the benefaction of your news of the world outside. And perhaps, in hearing of the pleasures of freedom, it will bring home to some of you the full significance of your internment here.' He gave me a quick slap round the head.

The letter trembled in my hand.

'Go on, boy! Read.'

The grey lines of boys in front of me waited in silence. There was not a snuffle, or a snigger. The bullying was shared by us all.

'Ah, the poor boy receives a letter from home, and cannot know what it says.' The Labour Master snatched the letter from me, and in a mocking tone, with a cynical twist, read it out. Everybody listened. And even the Labour Master's cruel way of reading, couldn't destroy the sound of Alice's gentle voice.

Dearest Arthur

I know that someone will read this for you. Perhaps one of the teachers who care for you will do so? We all miss you so much at home. The first evening you were gone, we laid a place for you at supper without thinking. And little Jenny kept looking for you and calling your name. Mother says at least it's good to know that the authorities are taking proper care of you and helping you.

The evenings are a little lighter now, though it's still cold.

Yours affectionately,
    Alice

At first it upset me that Alice believed I was living in some haven of peace with kind and caring teachers. But then I felt glad. It was best that way. I'd rather she and Ma had a reassuring image of life in Reform.

Alice wrote to me every week.

Dearest Arthur
We think of you every day though I'm afraid we no longer speak of you at home. Mother has put your boots to the back of the cupboard for it grieves her too much to see them. Remember that the Lord's Light is in *every* place. Where His love goes, there is light.

We have planted out the beans.

Your affectionate sister,
    Alice

The Labour Master quickly tired of his game of reading her letters aloud and Jamie was allowed to read to me instead.

Dearest Arthur
We'll all be thinking of you on Shrove Tuesday when we have the School Pancake Race. At least this year some of the other boys will stand a chance to win! We have sent a cake with the carrier. And please don't worry that we, at home, are going hungry on account of the cake. During Lent the Parish Fund has made an

allocation so that each family such as ours has the ingredients for a simnel cake for Easter. Mother and I made two, one for us and a smaller one for you.

Yours, very fondly,

Alice

I enjoyed her letter, though of course I never set eyes on any cake, nor did I dare ask after it. The Labour Master had clearly found a new way to punish me.

I kept all the letters hidden in a slit in my mattress so that, although I couldn't read them again, I could hold onto them at night in the dark, and feel the paper, and trace the black ink where Alice's pen had been.

After two or three readings by Jamie, I managed to learn most of the contents of each by heart and could repeat them to myself at night. The teacher in the Remedial Class said that there was nothing of any value inside my thick skull. Perhaps this was why I was able to retain so much of Alice's letters.

Dear Arthur

At last we've had the full story from Mr Pooley of how you were taken. Please, my dearest brother, don't let your spirit be broken. Remember how the rector used to teach us that Love must Triumph over all?

The weather has been Very Bad. Last night was quite wild, as dark as the grave Mother said. We'd already doused the fire and were on our way up when I heard a knocking outside. It was Mr Pooley, soaked through, water streaming off his hat, and down his shoulders, making puddles round him on the floor. He just stood, dripping, without saying anything at all. Then he said he was sorry. And he told Mother what a grim place it is you have gone to. I asked how long you're detained for, and he said it was six month. My poor Arthur. Six month is a long time for you.

Mother shook her head and said, Arthur won't like it, being closed up all the time. Arthur's always had the green in him.

And Mr Pooley said that if he'd only known it would end like this, he'd have acted different. Arthur, you've made everybody so sad. Why did you have to do it?

Alice

There was no message of love or affection at the end, and I didn't care for Jamie reading aloud such a letter. I didn't ask him to read it aloud a second time.

There were no more letters. I was worried. I fretted about it. I went over in my mind whether Alice had decided not to write. The Labour Master, knowing how much I relied on the weekly letters – for there were not many boys who had outside news so regularly – seemed triumphant. I began to suspect that he was deliberately withholding mail from me.

At last, I heard again.

Dearest Arthur

The weather has continued bad, just when we were hoping for Spring to stay. The sleet turned to snow. Mother says she can't remember a snowfall so late in spring. We've been snowed in this past four days. The lane was quite blocked, we couldn't get out for wood or food, nor down to the post. Each day, Mother said she hardly knew where the next meal was coming from. The creatures in the wood behind suffered the same way. There have been tracks in the snow all round the house, and I saw the fox right up at the window.

The snow is only lying on the fields now. Humphrey and I took Jenny down to school though she's not yet five, for Mother said it would be warmer there than to stay home. But when we reached school, we found it so cold that the ink was frozen in the pot.

The vegetable seedlings have been under snow for so

long I don't know if they will survive.

I have some other news, I hardly know if it's good or bad, but it may interest you. The rector's told me he's had his eye on me for some time and the petty post with his near relative is open again. A well-educated, well-spoken girl is needed. The rector is to write me good references. I know I must accept. The pay, Mother says, is very reasonable for an untrained girl. She'll be so glad of the money, and she tells me I *must* be grateful to all concerned, though really I suppose I must be grateful to YOU. I'm sure it's only on account of your arrest that they felt the necessity of finding me employment. In the village, they thought we'd all frozen to death at Pit Bottom during the snow. So we nearly had.

Mother feels great relief that I've a post so easily. I feel despair that I must leave school so soon, though I don't know when yet. I hope it won't be until after summer.

Your affectionate sister,
    Alice

I hardly slept that night. I was so relieved to have heard from her. I held the letter in my hand, while thoughts rushed round my head as though in a maze. I was forced to stay in school when I would rather leave. Alice, who wished to stay, must leave. There seemed no way out.

Dearest Arthur

This is my last week of school and you can guess how determined I am to enjoy every precious moment of it! Also, the last letter I'll write before I start with the Harkness family. They have the big square house beyond the village, it's about 2 mile. It's not a large household. They've no kitchen maid or underhouse-maid. As Between Maid, the duties of BOTH fall to me. I've a smart black dress, two white caps and aprons and

I'm to pay back the cost over the months out of my wage (£18 per year). I pay back one shilling a week for the cost of the laundry. I'd rather bring the uniform home to launder and save the shilling, but I'm afraid they don't care for that arrangement! I'll be able to write and tell you about my work once I've begun. As you can imagine, I'm quite frightened at the prospect in case I do anything wrong. Mr Pooley says that Mrs Harkness knows how I'm a keen reader and shouldn't be discouraged. He says I must try to keep up my reading. He has told me I'm to be awarded the year's Attendance Prize which is *Pilgrim's Progress* but I'm afraid I won't be there for the school Presentation.

Yours affectionately,

Alice

We were roused by the bell, routed out of bed, lined up in the dormitories, and marched down to the latrines. I tried to push my mind beyond the shouts and commands and frequent slaps of the Labour Master, and think of Alice scurrying over the open fields to be at her post by seven o'clock. However hard I tried to see her in a black dress and frilled cap, I could only see her in her short brown skirt, with a shawl and calico apron hurrying to school with yellow hair blowing across her eyes.

The dreariness of the next week was relieved by the expectation of hearing her account of life in employment. But then, suddenly, Jamie was taken ill, too ill to read to me. I could not ask any other boy to read instead. It was hard enough to share my glimpses of Alice and home with Jamie.

He had taken a bad beating for his continued bed-wetting. Every morning the straw in his palliasse was soaked right through, so that it even dripped onto the floor beneath. Every day, he had to parade round the yard with it tied to his back.

'This childish habit of persistent incontinence will be

stopped, if it's the last thing I do!' screamed the Labour Master.

Jamie was punished every day. The stripes on his back became infected. Lying in a wet bed at night, the infection quickly spread. He took a fever and became delirious. At last, he was moved to the Infirmary where a doctor attended to him. If he lived, we all expected that the Governors would send him home. For Jamie's sake, I hoped they would. For my own sake, I was glad when they did not.

He had a greyish complexion and a gauze dressing on his back when he returned to the main dormitory. I had three unread letters waiting.

Dear Arthur

On arrival, I was taken straight up to the drawing room to meet my employer. The rector had indeed given me good references. Mrs Harkness said that since I had the reputation of being a sensible and mature girl, she hoped I would honour the rector's generous expectation. And she said that if I show painstaking work, I may well rise to the top of the domestic ladder. But my duties are so numerous that it seems as though I haven't a moment to myself from when I arrive at daybreak, till when I sleep-walk home and fall into bed.

I have to begin with opening up the drawing room. They have both shutters *and* curtains. Then I sweep the breakfast room. I have to brush the dust *towards* the fire-place. They are most particular on that. I have to lay a cloth drugget over the carpet in front of the grate and have to put my housemaid's box on it, not beside it. There are so many utensils for polishing the grate! Black-lead brush, leathers, emery-paper, cloth. I have to work quietly as the household are still asleep when I arrive.

The housemaid checked the breakfast room after I'd finished, and showed me how to fold a piece of white paper and place it inside the grate against the polished bars, which gives a nice neat appearance. Coals and wood are laid *behind* so that they do not show.

Mrs Harkness was pleased with my first attempt at the paper fan. She even congratulated me. It quite made up for the scolding earlier.

Your affectionate sister,

Alice

The daintiness and the constant striving for cleanliness of Alice's work, contrasted strongly with the crudeness and squalor of life in Reform, although the drudgery of days were shared by us both. She began to sound quite disheartened.

As Betweenmaid, I also have to do kitchen work and prepare meat. They like to hang their poultry till it's quite high. When the smell is quite offensive it is my job to pluck and draw it. I told Cook I thought the meat was rotten. She turned on me quite sharply and said, 'Gentry like it ripe.' So now, when nobody is looking I take a piece of charcoal from the grates and place it in the vent of any bird left to hang to try and keep the flesh smelling sweet.

Cook doesn't like my appearance. She said it was time somebody 'did something' about my hair and asked if I had a hair brush. I said I had a comb, and was told, quite rudely, to use it!

The housemaid showed me how to twist the hair and pin it out of sight. But it will take days till I've mastered the art of keeping it pinned all day.

Your sister,

Alice

They had a preoccupation with hair in Reform School too. Our heads were clipped every week to lessen the incidence of lice, with which so many of us were infected.

I was in Reform the full six months. It seemed like a lifetime passing. Alice wrote every week. Only once, I wrote to her.

Dear Alice
I am to be relesed nex week. I have served my full six month. I do not know what I shall do on relese. I belive ther is a pass to see me hom. This letter is written for me by a friend, name Jamie.
Your brother,
Arthur Betts

Chapter 13

I STRODE up Pit Bottom Lane. Three rabbits scampered ahead of me, turned to stare with great eyes, like insolent children, then bobbed away with their white scuts turned up in fear.

The garden gate was more broken than I had remembered. It would need fixing before it quite fell off its hinges. But in the vegetable garden, Ma and Humphrey between them had grown a fine crop of beans, and the carrots were coming on well. I pulled one up by its fluffy green fronds, wiped off the earth and ate it raw.

I hummed merrily as I went up the path and into the cottage.

'Hello, Ma,' I said.

She was on her knees scrubbing. Little Georgina was up on the table out of the way of the wet. Ma looked round.

'So it's you? You're back?' she said.

She went on with the scrubbing, swishing the sand and water back and forth over the floor. Little Georgina hid her face in her skirt rather than look at me.

'You were expecting me, Ma, weren't you?' I said.

Ma nodded. 'We knew you'd be coming. Alice warned. Mind your boots on the bricks. Wait till I'm through.'

There was no smile of welcome. She finished the scrubbing at last, threw out the bucket of dirty water, and set Georgina down on the floor. She wiped her hands on her apron and came to give me a hug.

'Well, you've grown a bit taller now, Arthur,' she said,

with the smallest flicker of interest. 'Must be the plentiful food you had in Reformatory. You'll find we don't have much here. But we make do with what we can.' She spoke to me as though I were a stranger.

When Humphrey and Jenny ran in from school and saw me there, they stopped short in the doorway.

'Look, it's your brother back,' said Ma.

Humphrey grinned. Jenny stared.

'Where's Alice?' I asked.

'She's not back till late,' said Ma.

'The vegetables look good,' I said. 'You've done well.'

As my birthday fell in harvest time I would not have to go to school again, but my freedom from Reform did not last long. They had found me a probationary job as a cowherd. I didn't want to do it. But I knew I must.

I started work at four o'clock in the morning and I was to be paid a half salary until I had proved myself. I was to help with the dairy herd on one of his lordship's farms. I drove the cows into the parlour for first milking, I milked them, I drove them out to the meadow. I drove them back. I strained the milk into great wooden pails and carried them into the dairy. I cut up huge wads of fodder and carried them up to the meadows. I mucked out the milking parlour. I washed down the cows' hindquarters.

Alice and I were both out working twelve hours a day. She came back looking neat and fresh. I trudged back stinking of cow-dung. One evening, she was waiting for me in the gateway.

'Arthur,' she said. 'Why won't you talk to me any more, like we used to?'

I tried to squeeze past. I didn't want my milking apron to brush against her black dress. She stood firmly in the gateway and wouldn't let me through. She had all the obstinacy of our Pa.

'We never talked,' I said.

'Yes we did,' she said and her face flushed with anger. She

had all the quick temper of our Ma too. 'But now you aren't like a brother any more. Every time you come to this house, you're like a great cloud. You used to be funny and cheerful. You used to be my favourite brother.'

'You were always clever. I was always dull,' I muttered. 'Now let me pass,' I said and again tried to push through. 'I have to clean my boots.' I bent down and took them off. They were heavy with caked-on dirt. Alice snatched one of them out of my hand.

'*I'll* clean your boots for you,' she shouted. 'Just like I always have done, and you'll tell me what's wrong.'

'My life's finished, Alice,' I said. 'Yours is beginning, and mine's done.'

'Finished? Don't talk so stupid. They've given you a job, and a nice new pair of boots, and the ten shillings to start you off.'

'You don't know any of it, Alice. I've always been a dunce, I know that. I've been with beggar boys and thieves. They all think I've picked up bad ways. I'm changed. No one wants me round here, not even our Ma. The cowherd won't speak to me. I'm marked.'

Suddenly, without quite knowing why, I leant forward, rested my head on her shoulder and began to cry. Once started, it was hard to stop. 'I'm quite finished now,' I sobbed. 'It was terrible in Reform, like being dead all day, only not dying. Keeping on being dead, day after day.' I think she believed me because she didn't argue, just soothed. The sleeve of her maid's dress was all wet from my dripping nose.

'And everything's all right now, Arthur. You're out, and you've got a good job.'

'But why can't they give me a decent job?' I said. 'How can I be grateful for *this* job? They're stupid, slow, lazy brutes. Damn bitches, those cows.'

'Don't swear like that,' Alice said. 'Not where Mother can hear you.'

'I never was interested in cows. Nor never shall be. Can't even stand the taste of milk. Even ploughboy'd be better than this, driving them out to pasture, driving them back. They've no instinct, no grace. Just plod along through their own stinking sludge.' Alice wiped the mud off my boots with a handful of grass and brought them indoors to dry by the fire. Ma and Jenny were setting the table. Ma's face lightened at the sight of Alice.

I hung my milking apron, smelling of the cow-byre, on a hook in the shed.

I had blighted Ma's home. I could sense it. Alice was the favourite now. The little ways she had learned at Mrs Harkness, the vase of roses on the table, the clean cloth, the matching cups, all pleased our Ma.

It was too great a strain being at home. There was nothing but boredom being with cows. I wished I could go elsewhere. I wished I could get to keepering.

'My patience won't last,' I said to Alice. 'I can't be with the cows much longer. Standing around in slurry and straw all day long.'

'Gently, Arthur,' said Alice.

'I should be working in the woods,' I said. 'I know the woods. I know the birds. They put me in a job I can't stand on purpose.'

'You mustn't think you're working *against* them all the time. You're working *with* them.'

'Why can't I get to do keepering? Why can't I do what I want?'

'I passed Mr Pooley in the village,' said Alice. 'He said cows are good company when it's lonely for a boy out in the fields all day long.'

Mr Pooley knew nothing. He knew only about being stuffed indoors with books and learning.

'It's all under God's same sky, Arthur. With God's same creatures, birds or cows. And His good air to breathe.'

August was long and hot, like our first at Pit Bottom. The

weather brought a contentment to the village. On my way home from milking, I saw Mrs Craske open her window and sniff the evening air. But the endless sun and warm days also brought drought to the pastures. I had to cart water for the herd on a barrow up from the farm three times a day.

Alice had the fourth Sunday in August off, so I tried to get home to have dinner with the family. She brought back a bit of leftover beef. There wasn't much of it, only a scraping of shin, but it went well with the vegetables. We hadn't had meat for a long time, though there was plenty of it round about, plenty of rabbits too. But I wasn't going out after any of it.

Ma was suspicious about the shreds of beef she found in the stew. She thought *I* had put the meat in with the vegetables.

'Where d'you get it, Arthur? You stolen it? You been up to your tricks?' she asked.

'No, Mother, I brought it. It was a gift from Cook. She said too much went to waste as it was, up there,' said Alice.

The warm weather had dried out the damp thatch of Pit Bottom. After dinner, Humphrey and I carried the kitchen bench outside so that Ma and Alice could sit in the sun. They rested their backs against the crumbly wall where it was warm. I thought a bit of sun might soften Ma up a bit.

'Pa's roses look good,' said Alice.

Ma nodded. 'First ones came out right at the start of June.' The briar that Pa had planted was blooming all round the door and had reached right up to the chimney.

Alice took Jenny onto the bench beside her and taught her how to plait her hair.

'You'll save Ma the trouble every morning before school,' Alice said. 'And I'll buy you some ribbon if you're good.' Then Alice took little Georgina on her lap and began to teach her her letters. Alice always had to be busy doing something, or teaching somebody something. But Georgina grew bored quickly. She didn't want to know about her

C-A-T and H-A-T and M-A-T. She slid off Alice's lap, and skipped away to play.

There was a sudden commotion down in the lane, breaking up the drowsy afternoon. A gang of boys up from the village were yelling my name as they came rushing up towards the cottage.

'Betts! Betts! Are you there?' Samuel Dix had been at Pooley's school the same time as me.

He ran along the other side of the hedge calling at me through the leaves.

'War! Betts, war! There's going to be a war!'

Three lads crowded in through the gate, bright with excitement. I went across the garden to meet them.

'We're all going to volunteer! Take the King's Shilling down at Reepham Market. Next Thursday.'

Ma, woken by the noise, came over.

'Arthur?' she asked sharply. 'Why're these boys here? What kind of trouble are you in now? If the cowherd catches you –'

'It's a war, ma'am,' said Samuel Dix. 'We're all going to sign on. We were asking Betts if he'd come too.'

'What sort of war?' Our Ma didn't read. She didn't concern herself with village gossip. War was the topic of old men, deaf and with knobbly knuckles who talked about the Boers.

'The Huns are coming, Mrs. When they get here, they'll burn down the trees, kill all the cattle, murder his lordship in his bed, and make all the children into slaves!' said Samuel Dix.

One of the other lads nodded encouragement. 'It's true. They're recruiting Thursday fortnight. We're all going. They'll be giving out the uniforms and guns. And paying us the privilege.'

'You're all too young,' Alice joined in. 'Arthur can't go, Ma. Tell him he can't go.'

I wasn't even sure I wanted to yet.

'Will you come with us then, Betts?'

I shrugged. 'I'm not sure,' I said. 'I got to go now. Back for the evening milking. Cows don't pray Sundays, worst luck.' I hurried off to the pasture to drive my herd in, leaving Alice and the three boys arguing by the gate. She had known each of them in school, heard their lessons, taught them sums and wiped their slates.

There was a full harvest moon when I walked home that night, rising red over the stubblefields. I heard a fox barking, and a screech owl calling. I had never been afraid of the dark. But if what the boys said was true, when the Huns came, others might be. They would not be safe at night. Nobody would be able to walk freely.

On recruiting day, we all put our ages on a bit. Few of us could read and write. When it came to giving the birth date for filling in the forms and documents, we mumbled our way through.

The recruiting officer looked down at me a bit suspicious. But I managed to pass for sixteen by standing tall and holding out my chest.

When Humphrey saw my uniform, the khaki tunic with shiny buttons, the belt, the puttees to wind round my legs, and the great breeches hanging loose and large, he wanted to be a soldier too. But he still had a soft skin like a baby and a high voice. There was no way he could pass for more than thirteen at most.

All the men of the neighbourhood who had enlisted were to be invited by his lordship to a Soldiers' Tea. You had to inform the housekeeper that you wished an invitation.

I had never seen the big house close to, only from a distance through the trees. But I didn't go to the Soldiers' Tea though Alice urged me hard enough. I was too shy.

'Go *on*, Arthur! They say he's got over a hundred rooms there. I'd do anything to have a peek.'

I heard afterwards from Samuel Dix that I wouldn't have seen inside any of the hundred rooms anyway. They held the tea round the back, outside his lordship's stables.

Before we went to join our regiments, I gave Humphrey my catapult, and my store of horse-hair snares.

'Look after them,' I said. 'Use them carefully, and don't get took, or I'll give you a hiding when I'm back.'

Humphrey slipped the catapult into his pocket, and the snares went back under a loose brick.

'What about the other? Where's it hid? I'll look after it for you,' he said.

I shook my head. 'No, sorry, Humphrey. It's coming with me.' I didn't know if I could, but I thought I'd have a try.

Everybody knew all along I'd got Pa's gun hidden somewhere about. I buttoned up my tunic, put on my cap and went out to fetch it. For once, there was no secrecy. The family followed me down the lane. I stopped a hundred yards from our gate. They watched as I plunged my hand into a hollow tree and pulled out the long sacking package.

'You're not taking your Pa's shotgun to shoot the enemy?' our Ma asked, suddenly smiling. 'Oh, you are a lovely lovely boy!' She flung her arms round my neck and hugged me. It was the first time she'd shown any affection for me since I was back from Reform. When I was fully dressed up in my uniform, she hovered round me half laughing, half crying.

'Oh, you do look so fine, Arthur my darling. If only your Pa could see what a fine darling you are.' But I'm sure she was glad I was going away.

We laughed and sang our way along the lanes to the railway station. It was like a gypsy parade. Jenny and Georgina skipped in front. Humphrey tried marching in step with me. Soon there was quite a crowd of us, growing bigger at almost every cottage we passed, for so many of us had joined up.

Some of the old men came too, wearing their medals pinned to their coats. I caught sight of Jo Plumb, though I wouldn't look him in the eye. He too wore medals on his chest, though I don't believe he ever won them.

As we rounded a bend in the lane and reached the station I felt my stomach sink like lead.

'You're not afraid, are you?' Alice whispered in my ear. 'Of war?'

'Of course not,' I said, and tried to make my feet march on. 'But over there –'

It was not just us cottage labourers who'd volunteered. A waggon pulled up in front of the station with numbers of the estate workers too.

I saw Mr Wilkins and Mrs Wilkins, with their son Wilfrid.

My feet dragged. I swung the gun down from my shoulder and carried it low at my side. But it gleamed brightly. The barrels and lock were shiny and well kept.

The other volunteers and their families surged ahead onto the platform. Humphrey and Jenny, Alice, Ma, and little Georgina clustered round me protectively. But Mr Wilkins had seen me. He strode over, his big red hand outstretched to me as though we were equals. My own hand was weighted to my side, unable to move. Alice nudged me. 'Shake hands, you idiot!' she hissed. 'You look so ill-mannered.'

'Well done, lad. You're all brave boys,' said Wilkins. Then he walked back to his party.

Instructed by his father, Wilkins' son came over too. He too had a shotgun with him. Stiffly, we shook hands, but said nothing.

The train slid into the station hissing out steam. We clambered on board.

Chapter 14

So we all went gloriously off to fight our war, leaving behind our families to get on with their mundane lives. But army life, too, was hard. Some of the boys had never before been away from their homes. They baulked at the discipline. They suffered severe homesickness. But for me it was less confining than I had expected and I found that I settled quickly to the life.

As there was a shortage of service rifles, Wilfrid Wilkins and I kept our guns with us. This made us the envy of some of the other lads who had to make do with wooden dummies for practice drill. Our knowledge of ammunition proved useful too, and Wilf Wilkins and I quickly became the best of pals, along with Bessie Godfrey's brother. Our Brigade even came to be known as the Gamekeeper's Rifles, for so many of our number were from the land. I felt that I had, at last, become a keeper of sorts.

Though many of us were no more than boys, we were treated as men, fed as men, called men, and we were paid a man's wage.

But things did not work out quite as I had planned. Not only my youth, but my lack of education was soon revealed. They did not post me to the front. Instead, I endured the frustration of garrison service at home. I fretted at this, for the war would be over by Christmas, so they said, and then I should have missed it altogether.

We ineducables spent our mornings cleaning and maintaining artillery and our afternoons in a classroom. I did not know, till then, that there was a special word for the likes of me. I was illiterate. Our teacher was the regiment's chaplain, Father Pawlby, whose contribution to the war effort was the spread of literacy. His role was not to go over the top and be shot to bits but to teach us to read and write so that, once literate, we might be sent over the top.

'Learning to read,' said Father Pawlby at our first lesson, 'is a wonderful achievement. It elevates us above God's creatures. I have been surprised and saddened by the great number in our ranks who are here, termed ineducable. But you are not imbeciles, nor idiots.'

I had always had the sense that my inability to learn, was my own failing, was due to my own limitations.

'Rather,' the chaplain went on, 'it seems to me, that many of you received your tuition too seldom and of the wrong kind. I have a simple explanation. Till now, you have been badly taught.'

He did not treat me with contempt or ridicule. Instead, he gave me time. He dispelled the panic, the fear in the pit of the stomach when presented with a page of text.

'It is only a matter of gaining confidence. You are all perfectly capable, intellectually, of mastering literacy. You are not children. If you have the maturity to volunteer to serve your country, you have within you the confidence to master reading.'

It was, at first, so hard. I really wanted to succeed, and yet was not able. The printed bookpage was lifeless. The letter shapes on the paper sat there, without order or meaning, though sometimes jigging up and down before my gaze, seeming to shift in their order like small insects.

There was the confusion of *d* and *b*, of *g* and *j*, and *p* and *q*. What was the difference between *D* and *O*, or *B* and *R*? What the meaning of *sh* and *ch*? Why the *e* which made no sound, yet appeared at the right hand end of so many word shapes? *Bed, deb, good, god* and *dog* seemed all so similar, yet their sound and meaning was intended to be different.

When I heard some of the other illiterates read, jerkily, stilted, without confidence, as though they did not know what they read, I knew that I was the same. We would none of us ever gain that smooth sweet murmur that Alice had.

At first I would rush at each page to get done quickly, only to flounder and stumble within a moment so that the words could have no meaning. Now, gradually, I began to know when to pause, and when to carry on, for the chaplain taught us the meaning of the commas, and the full stops along the line.

'Accept them,' he said. 'They're not there to trick you but to help you find the sense.'

The chaplain did not use a primer full of sat, mat, hat and fat. Instead, he read aloud to us a great deal, chiefly from the Psalms of which he seemed particularly fond.

'O be joyful in the Lord, all ye Lands. O sing unto the Lord a new song,' he shouted out at us as though we were assembled in church. I knew many of the verses from the evenings at home when Alice used to read aloud. But Father Pawlby's voice was nowhere as lovely as hers. After the Bible, he gave us practice with words we might use in our daily life, the words of objects we saw around – barracks, rifle, waggon, breeches, parade ground. And the words too, of those things we could not see, but knew were there – anger, hope, despair, and friendship.

His instruction classes were no game, yet some of his techniques seemed like a game. To each lad, he gave one letter of the alphabet and a printed report of a recent manoeuvre, and we must seek out the words which began with our given letter.

Mine was B. What a list I found. I had no idea at that time of their meaning, but I was triumphant when I could search out a handful that did indeed begin with my letter, even when at times it was B, and at others, b: battalion, blighty, brigade, British, Bertha, brass, Belgium, baccy, brass, boots, bully beef, buttons, Beer Coy, Batt, Bolo, BTO, BEF, Bovril, Bourlon Wood, Bailleul, Bapaume.

This was not a trial or punishment, but a demanding and exhilarating exercise. I was dizzy with surprise at my own achievement.

I concentrated on the learning to read. I thought if I got over that, I could get on with the spelling and the writing after. And suddenly, the reading came. The realization that I had mastered it came in an instant, in the mess.

I turned to pass a remark to one of my fellows along the bench when my eye was caught by a small coloured picture lying on the floor beneath the table. It was a cigarette card, showing a lapwing egg. At least, it looked like a lapwing egg from its slightly pointed end, and its dark blotched camouflage. I picked up the card, idly turned it over. On the reverse, at the top, in bold print, were two words, *Lapwing Egg*, and beneath in smaller, close, print was written: 'The Lapwing's nest is difficult to locate. It is sparsely lined, often hidden in a hollow on the ground, or in a grassy tussock. The Lapwing lays four eggs. It makes its home in marshes, meadows, moors and fields. It is easily identified by its thin crest. In cold weather, large flocks may be seen in movement from one locality to another.'

I was astounded to find that I had followed all this with ease. So I went through it again, and again, till I had nearly memorized it.

Several of the lads collected cigarette cards. I quickly found a soldier who had a full set entitled *British Birds and Their Eggs*, telling of the curlew, the guillemot, the great auk, the raven, stonechat, and many more. He was more concerned with the number of sets he could amass than in the information contained on them. He had full sets covering *Racehorses*, *Flags*, and *Naval Vessels*. There was a new set, *Military Motors*, which was so popular that he only managed to collect two of the cards.

He allowed me to borrow each of his sets. The ones I

enjoyed most were those on Natural History. Much of the writing about Fish, Wild Flowers, and Butterflies I knew already in my mind, but had never before seen set out in words. I knew, for instance, dozens of the butterflies by sight and habitat yet never before had known their different names, for up till now, I had learned only what I saw with my eyes or gathered from my own experience. All other information had been rationed. But now, I could know anything I wanted. I had found a freedom that went with me, inside my head.

I had a bit of a try at *Comic Cuts* and the *Daily Graphic*, and the pocket Testament given me by the chaplain, but of all the matter available, I most preferred the cards. The illustration on one side told what meaning you were looking for, and the text gave exactly the information you needed.

After that, in the ineducables' class, even where there was no picture as guidance, the words fell together, tumbling off the page in coherent sequence.

But the writing came harder. I wrote my letters small and cramped so that, even when they were often wrong, it might give an impression of a word. The chaplain told me instead to write them big and separate, like a babies' alphabet chart. When I made a mistake with these big bold letters, I could see it myself and correct it. And in the end, I mastered the writing too and was dismissed from literacy class.

The war did not end at Christmas, and I was home for three days' leave before we were to sail for France.

As I stepped into Pit Bottom cottage, a curious thing happened. I suddenly seemed to see it as others must have seen it, as my family really were – poor and dirty. The kitchen looked little better than Mrs Craske's hovel, with the curtains so shabby, the floor so uneven and grimed, even though dear Ma tried hard enough.

'Ma, they have taught me the writing and reading,' I said, as I kissed her.

She stood there with her cracked hands clasped against

her apron and I felt ashamed of her ignorance, and her stupid delight at having a uniformed soldier in her kitchen. In the time that I had been away, she seemed to have grown old.

'I can't say we're sorry you've not been posted to the front,' said Alice as she set the table. 'We've heard that the young men there have such a hard time of it. Cook's cousin has already been injured. Though he's not bad.'

In the evening when the young ones had gone up, Alice and I sat and enjoyed the fire a while longer. Ma dozed in her chair, with her feet up on the fender.

'Mrs Harkness wants me to move back to London with them, as housemaid,' said Alice.

'And will you go?'

She nodded. 'The wage is much increased. And a room to myself, and all board.'

'We're going foreign, too,' I said. 'So it's rumoured.'

I had not told Ma. I glanced over to see if she had heard, but she was asleep with her chin dropped down to her chest.

'Will you write to me, about how it is over there?' Alice asked.

'Of course,' I said. 'If you do.'

She hugged me good night. 'Then take care, Arthur,' she said.

I didn't see her in the morning, for she had already left for work by the time I was awake.

We crossed the channel on the deck of a rusty steamer. We were landed in Le Havre, and after one night's rest, were loaded onto open railtrucks and delivered to the base camp. This was still some way from the front, with pleasant woods around, a slow moving stream, and avenues of poplar trees. On the first night, I stood out in a little oak wood on a slight hill, and I saw the yellow and white flickering on the horizon, and heard the muffled sound of distant gunfire. At last, I was in the war.

Alice wrote regularly, of the cheerful goings-on in her

new London household, of the young man who had the cheek to deliver Mrs Harkness' pork chops to the front door, of the kitchen maid's attempt to pluck a hen. And I told her of the boisterous sporting activities of my fellow men.

'The sergeant and I went scrumping in the village,' I wrote. 'Yesterday we took a goose from the Frenchies from right under an old woman's nose. It was so Fat we could have done with Roast Apples to go in him.'

The following month, I had to write and tell her how the Frenchies had taken to locking up their fowl at night, and sometimes even took them indoors with them, right into their homes, those that still had homes. For we soon saw that these country folk were not just poor as we, at home, had been poor. They were watching their whole livelihood, their farms, and their landscape blasted away before their eyes. Sometimes, they passed us on the long straight roads, fleeing from their bombarded villages. So no more goose.

Instead, some of the lads tried to catch pigeon, without much success. I wrote and told Alice how I had set to thinking of the best way, which was to make the bird drunk. I took some brandy which the Lieutenant had for first-aid purposes, and soaked some corn in the brandy. The birds came for the corn and were soon so drunk that they tottered about and fell down on their sides, so we could pick them up quite easily, and had a feast.

Soon after that, we moved our position. Up at the front there were no birds, indeed no life of any sort. The trees were all shot bare, and the ground frozen mud and wire, with no corner for any bird to hide. Sometimes I longed to see a bit of wild life, just to know that the world we were fighting for was still going.

On a quiet night, Wilf Wilkins and I were sent out on a sortie into no man's land. We blundered about in the dark, lost all sense of direction, and could not find our way back. In the end we tumbled into a shell crater to wait for first light in the hopes of then determining our position better. We were very cold. Our greatcoats, already sodden, froze as stiff as boards, as we lay together waiting.

At dawn, we saw that a thin white mist covered everything. It was this which had confused us in the night, for it distorted both vision and sound. There was an eerie stillness and we still did not know which way to go. Then the sun came through the mist making it glow red, dispersing some of the vapour, and glinting on fragments of cracked ice. The devastated scene became a still world of grey and gold.

Wilf slithered to the top of our crater and cautiously peered over.

'I think I've got it,' he whispered. 'We've come too far that –' I never heard which way we had come too far for as he spoke a shell burst a few yards from our burrow. I closed my eyes, and drew up my knees. For a moment I forgot where we were. When I opened my eyes I saw that his tin hat, his ear, and half his head were blown away.

Heavy shelling went on throughout the day. I lay beside Wilkins' body until evening when I made it back to our trenches and the stretcher party collected his body.

After that, I stopped writing to Alice for there was nothing more to say. I could not write to her of the rats, or the lice or the pervading smell, nor of the dragging boredom which alternated with patches of acute fear. Her prattling letters, moreover, no longer amused me. Her war, with its knitting of blanket squares, its relief committees, shortage of fresh chicken, and excitement of spotting a Zeppelin, seemed a different war from mine.

So it was simply a matter of enduring, as once I had endured Reform School, just a matter of closing one's mind and surviving until either one was shot or the war ended, whichever came first.

Chapter 15

SHORTLY before the armistice, I heard that Ma had died of bronchitis. I sent money for the funeral expenses. Alice wrote that Jenny and Georgina had been taken by the rector's wife to the St Mary Home for little children, and that Humphrey was to be sent as labourer to work for a Mr Bussins.

When we were demobbed, I went first to find Alice in London.

'You were right not to go back to Pit Bottom,' Alice told me. 'There's no point. I dare say the old place has even fallen down by now.'

She was doing well for herself, two maids under her, and still courted by the butcher's son.

'I've been fooling myself all along when I thought I could be the saviour of the family,' she said. 'We can do nothing now but stick together and save each other. We must put the place we grew up entirely from our minds.'

'You're going up in the world,' I said.

'I'll say so.'

'Always on the razzle-dazzle. You and your Ed. If you play your cards right I suppose you'll get a proposal any day now.'

Alice's employers were good people. They let me sleep in the press off the kitchen, and gave me odd jobs about the place until such a time as I found work and lodgings of my own.

'I think they want to repay the debt for the many who

died,' said Alice. 'Mr Harkness had no sons to volunteer, only girls.'

Ed, the butcher's son, came for Alice on Sunday afternoons. Alice's employer let her go provided she was accompanied by one of the other maids, or by myself. Ed and Alice liked to go up West on the tram, and stroll along by the river.

'Where's it to be, Al?' Ed liked to call her Al. He thought it was classy.

'Westminster Abbey,' she said. 'Arthur and I are going to visit the new tomb.'

In the kitchen, the servants had been talking about it. The Tomb of the Unknown Warrior. The King had just unveiled the stone. Inside was supposed to lie the body of an unnamed soldier who had died in battle. His name and regiment were said to be lost so that nobody knew who it was in there.

'You lost somebody then, Al?' asked Ed.

'Everybody's lost *somebody*!' Alice said.

'My brother went. He'd have gone into the business. I know I should grieve but how can I when I hardly knew him? And I'll get the whole firm to myself?'

We had to queue for over an hour to get into the Abbey, shuffling forward a few steps at a time. Police constables were stationed along the pavement to watch that the crowd waited tidily. The silent sombre line stretched out of the west doors, along the railing and round past the Houses of Parliament for half a mile or more.

The tomb wasn't much to look at, just a flat black marble stone set into the floor, with a Union Jack draped over and a spray of cotton poppies. Four white candles burned on each corner, and four soldiers, with reversed bayonets stood guard. I noticed many people cry as they passed, but I didn't feel the need.

When our turn came, we paused for a second and stared down at the flag under which lay the mangled remains of some boy, or brother, or father or man.

Alice dropped a threepenny bit into a collecting box on the way out.

'Why d'you do that?' I asked.

'Pay for the candles,' Alice said. 'They'll keep the candles lit always, long after we're gone. It's nice to think of candles burning over him for ever, don't you think?'

She spoke of the soldier as though he were whole. I had seen enough to know that it was probably only bits of a man. As we came out of the oppressive gloom into Parliament Square, a faint breeze ruffled the leaves of a plane tree to reveal a pigeon preening itself on a branch. It turned its head and seemed to gaze directly at me, then cooed as though it were alone in secluded woodland. I felt a yearning for the countryside, for the innocence and freedom of boyhood.

'If only I'd got to keepering, like I always wanted.'

'Keepering's a mug's game, Arthur. No future in it.' *She* was going to be a London butcher's wife. She was already accustoming herself to pleasant ways.

'I could've been a fine keeper. I know I could, if only I'd been given the chance.'

'Yes, and you might just as easily have ended up a Joseph Plumb. Ignorant, illiterate and on the run for the rest of your life.'

'If only I'd caught it in France, like the rest of them. Wilkins gone. Samuel Dix. Bessie Godfrey's brother. All gone.'

'If only! If only!' Alice suddenly turned on me. 'It's no good if-onlying for the rest of your life,' she snapped. 'You've got to grow up and see the world that's here now.'

'That's all very well for you,' I said. 'You'll end up a butcher's wife, in business with our fine young friend here. What am I left with? What have I got out of it all?'

'There'll be something for you. For certain there will.'

Ed hovered uncertainly beside us, excluded from our argument.

'Tea, Al?' he said tentatively. 'Up the 'Dilly? Tea and cinnamon toast and a plate of fancy cakes? You too, Arthur.'

'Thank you, Ed,' said Alice. 'We're just coming.'

She linked her arm firmly through mine so that I was forced to walk with her. Ed took her other arm.

Suddenly Alice grinned at me. 'D'you remember Bessie Godfrey's brother in class, the way he used to hum through his nose and make us all giggle? It used to drive poor old Pooley half wild.'

Already Alice had turned our childhood into a bright and happy dream.

GO WELL, STAY WELL
Toeckey Jones

Hamba kahle – Go well, stay well – is the Zulu phrase to wish a friend a safe journey, and one of the many things Candy learns from Becky. But had an accident not brought them together, they might never have met – never mind become such good friends. For although they live in the same South African city, their lifestyles could not be more different. While Candy's family have a large, comfortable house in the suburbs of Johannesburg, Becky lives in the black township of Soweto.

From the moment of their meeting, Candy and Becky realise just how difficult it is going to be to remain friends. The laws of apartheid that restrict meetings between blacks and whites put all number of obstacles in their way, and it is only their instinctive liking of one another that gives them the determination to fight for the right to share each other's company as equals.

Set in South Africa in 1976, this honest novel portrays the tensions and difficulties of that society and the feelings of many young people growing up there today.